The Lies in the Lefse

A Cash Kristiansen Mystery: #2

George Robstad

from various sources. Please consult a licensed professional before attempting any techniques outlined in this book.

By reading this document, the reader agrees that under no circumstances is the author responsible for any losses, direct or indirect, that are incurred as a result of the use of the information contained within this document, including, but not limited to, errors, omissions, or inaccuracies.

Cash Kristiansen Mysteries

Book 1: Sandbakkels & Sin

Book 2: The Lies in the Lefse

Table of Contents

Chapter 1

Cash Kristiansen sat in his inherited rinky-dink SUV, staring out at the parking lot of the Fjord & Fika. His hands still rested on the leather steering wheel, picking at loose pieces of it with one nail.

Just an hour earlier, he'd had his sixth session with Irene, the island's only therapist. She was intelligent and helpful, but Cash's heart still felt heavy at the sight of the patisserie in front of him. He found himself wishing that his aunt Sigrid could still have been here, that he could meet her inside and have one more simple meal. These were thoughts that he'd had often, and ones he didn't think he could ever escape.

This is it, he thought, watching the clouds in the distance slowly crawl across the bright sky.

For years, his view had been obscured by skyscrapers and the noise of the city. Cash still couldn't quite get used to the mild buzzing of life on Salt Cliff Isle, the low hum that had become music to his ears.

The SUV's door creaked open with its rusty hinges as Cash stepped out into the salty air, a smile on his face and a bittersweetness in his heart. If it hadn't been for what had happened to Sigrid, he would have likely visited and then returned to the city. Life would have moved on as it always did, fast-paced and stressful. He wouldn't have the new friends that he did now, nor the life that now lay ahead of him.

Even so, Cash still would have wanted Sigrid to be there instead in a heartbeat if he'd had the choice.

Around him, the world was still somewhat quiet, the sun still low in the sky. There was the sound of island birds in the trees that lined the edges of the parking lot, and the far-off grumble of the ocean, and the crunch of Cash's shoes on the rocks beneath his feet.

He took a deep breath and turned to face the patisserie. It was silent, as it had been for the month since Sigrid's funeral, as if it was waiting to be awoken once again. The keys to the front door jingled in Cash's pocket as he began to walk closer. There was a single moment of doubt that crossed his mind; a question of whether he could truly make a success of this the way that Sigrid had.

She had been a legend on the island for many years, a cornerstone of its culture. Her passion for the food she made was infectious, and, on top of that, she'd had a hand in much of the island's architecture before she retired.

But Cash simply shook his head at himself. *You're prepared. You can do this.*

He was ready for this new chapter in his life. It was a new beginning, a welcome change that he had been longing for for years—something he'd only realized when he'd returned to the island. Perhaps the realization could have happened under easier circumstances, but he was grateful for it nonetheless.

"Hey!" Amelia's chipper voice sounded out from behind him. She was flanked by Brian and Selena, who both wore bright smiles and the kind of excitement that came along with weeks of anticipation.

They had all worked under Sigrid and knew the patisserie well; even Amelia, who was the newest of the employees, had a great love for the place. Cash knew that he'd have the best in the business at his side, and that he'd be able to learn everything he needed to know from them and the recipes that Sigrid had left behind.

Cash nodded at them and pulled the keys to the front doors from his pocket. "You guys ready for this?"

He received a pair of happy grins from Brian and Amelia and a far more committed and serious nod from Selena. She crossed her arms and stared at the front door as if she were a captain preparing to sail through a storm.

"I can't believe so much time has passed already," she remarked, letting her eyes run across the front of the building. "It feels like the mayor was arrested just yesterday."

"Yeah, it's a little weird," Amelia added, tapping at her chin. "But I'm so glad we get to work again. I was running out of things to do. You can only binge-watch so many things before you lose your mind."

"Speak for yourself," Brian joked with a mild chuckle.

"Right, let's do it," Cash laughed, somewhat shakily raising the key to unlock the door. His heart was beating quickly as it clicked and swung open with a welcoming *woosh.* As he stepped inside, he was greeted by the familiar cozy warmth of the patisserie's decor, even without the lights, people, and smell of baked food.

The light blue and white walls and wooden tables felt like coming home, even if the pillows weren't quite as puffy as usual, and though there was some dust over everything. Cash made a mental note of everything that needed to be fixed up before they opened.

"Oh, I can't wait to see my regulars again," Brian said as he hopped past Cash and toward the back. "Some of them tip *really* well, you know?"

Amelia laughed, already lighting up the space with pure personality. "Honestly, I'm jealous. I haven't even had the chance to really get some proper regulars yet."

"You will," Selena answered encouragingly, placing one hand on Amelia's shoulder. "I mean, we all had to start somewhere."

From there, Selena busied herself with making the booths and tables look nice, while Amelia worked on getting the register ready, and Cash moved to his office. He unlocked the door with a heart that was slightly heavy. He wished that Sigrid could have been here with him, but he knew that she would have been happy knowing that her passion was still being kept alive. He thought for a moment about trying out architecture, too, but shook his head at himself. He'd never been good at drawing in the first place, and with how technical architecture was, he didn't quite think it'd be down his alley.

The office was waiting for him with the efficient preparations he'd made; a simple desk with only a laptop and files along the shelving against the wall. He had brought a few personal things with him to make the space more his own. A photo of him with Sigrid, a notebook, and a pen cup shaped like a seagull that he'd found in one of the small shops along the beach road. He had more plans, but he was starting slow. He had the rest of his life to create his own place on the island, after all.

Cash put everything away and took a seat on the rolling office chair behind the desk. Things were quiet now, but he knew that everything would pick up soon. The whole town had been humming with the news about the patisserie's reopening, and Cash had no doubt that the first customers would be lining up soon.

"Hey!" Amelia threw open the office door brightly. "Why don't we have a celebratory batch of Sandbakkels before things get crazy?"

Cash raised one eyebrow, amused. "You know what? That's not a terrible idea. Get the others."

He stretched himself out and took one more look at his new desk before he got to his feet and headed to the kitchen. He could feel the life slowly coming back to the patisserie, with every joke from Brian, every laugh from Amelia, and every bemused shake of the head from Selena.

"Right," Cash said once they'd all gathered on either side of one of the kitchen islands and the chatter had subsided. "Do you all still remember your parts, or do you need a refresher?"

He'd hidden Sigrid's recipes in her house and memorized every single one meticulously. Each section had been assigned to one of the employees individually, so that nobody actually knew the entire thing. Exactly the way Sigrid had done it. Cash had been thinking of ways that he could make the patisserie all his own, but this... this he would keep as it was.

"Mm," Amelia murmured as she tapped at her chin. "I *think* I know my bit."

Selena clicked her tongue. "One month and you're already a blank slate."

"Maybe we should go over it just once," Brian said, his cheeks slightly red. "Couldn't do any harm, could it?"

Cash nodded slowly before he had each of them individually repeat their sections to him outside of the kitchen. Once he was happy with every process, he sent them off to their stations, and they got started. Cash himself kept a watchful eye, noting each step in his mind and matching it to his memories of Sigrid's recipes.

Soon enough, the kitchen filled with the sweet smells of baking, a scent that had been missing from the place for far too long. Knowing that it would hang in the air again every day had Cash smiling to himself. A few weeks earlier, he had wondered if it was the right decision to stay on Salt Cliff. But now, he was completely convinced. He could barely imagine himself ever returning to the city again.

Being here made him feel as if there was finally somewhere that he could truly belong. He already had a solid group of friends, even though he hadn't known most of them for very long. His little routine had grown on him, and despite running around to get everything ready for the Fjord & Fika to open again, he hadn't been this relaxed in years. Frankly, he barely recognized the person he had been five mere weeks earlier.

"Ah, get it in the oven!" Amelia was shrieking in the background, as if a delay of a few seconds would ruin the entire batch. In all fairness, that was something Sigrid would have believed, too. There was a reason she'd chosen these three as her employees. Despite her kindness and how relaxed she often seemed, Cash was well aware that there were areas in Sigrid's life where she was a fairly rigid perfectionist.

Selena rushed past Cash with the entire batch, hurriedly arranging it in the oven before closing it up and breathing a sigh of relief. They all took a moment to calm down.

All four of them stood staring at the oven together in a huddle, as if that would make it bake faster. On one counter stood the timer, the seconds ticking by the only sound in the room aside from the low hum of the oven itself. Cash could feel the excitement building in his chest. He wondered if he would ever truly get used to this, or if that sensation of pure contentment would fade.

Maybe it wouldn't, and maybe that was why Sigrid built the patisserie in the first place. Cash had never had an intense passion like that, something that could take over his entire life and drive him toward a particular future. But perhaps he was going to find it here, and that possibility was carrying him now.

"It's almost time," Brian said, leaning forward as if he were reading some sort of prophecy. "Come on... We've been waiting for this for *so* long."

"True," Selena agreed, moving aside to allow Brian to do his part of the recipe. "We were so used to getting baked stuff every day. It was like living in a desert the last few weeks."

Cash felt slightly bad about that. He had been practicing several of Sigrid's recipes at home, so much so that he'd had to give some of the results away to friends and neighbors. But he hadn't thought about giving any of it to Brian, Selena, or Amelia. He made a small note in his mind to try to connect more with them. Sigrid had gotten fairly close to them all before her death; it was only right for him to try to do the same.

The timer rang, and Brian immediately got to work removing the sandbakkels from the oven and getting them ready to cool down. Finally, they were all standing around the kitchen island, staring at the batch standing atop it in an ornate plate as Selena carefully filled them with a sour cherry filling.

"Honestly, I think Sigrid would have been proud of this one," Brian said, a glint of nostalgia burning in his eye, and he even wiped a small tear from his cheek. "I miss her so much."

"Me, too," Cash admitted, struggling to keep his own stoic expression on his face for a moment.

Selena reached for the plate and grabbed a sandbakkel. "To Sigrid! And to Fjord and Fika!"

Her words broke the building somber mood, and they all reached for their own cookie, clinking them together like glasses and cheering.

Biting into his own sandbakkel, Cash was immediately aware that this batch was far better than any of the practice runs he'd made over the past few weeks. It was a good thing he didn't have to run the patisserie entirely on his own.

Once they'd all finished eating, there were only about twenty minutes left before they were supposed to open. In a flurry of limbs and talking, Amelia, Selena, and Brian rushed to get the last bits and pieces in place while Cash opened the register and moved himself to the door to greet the first arriving customers.

A line was already forming in front of the door, with people talking in excited whispers and peering through the windows.

"Morning," Cash said as he stepped outside, his brightest customer-service smile crossing his face. "We're almost ready for you. Thank you for your patience."

Someone pushed past most of the group and stepped up to Cash with an outstretched hand. He seemed familiar, though Cash couldn't place him immediately. His hands were rough, as if he'd done a lot of manual labor in his life, and he was tanned; the kind of man who spent a lot of time in the sun.

"Name's Orin," he said as Cash shook his hand. "I wanted to talk to you about the upcoming mayoral event at the brewery."

Behind Cash, Brian was opening the doors to the public and customers hurried inside to find a spot.

"Uh, I'm not running," Cash said awkwardly to Orin as he ran a hand through his hair.

"No, no, certainly," Orin laughed, almost like the suggestion was one of the most ridiculous things he'd ever heard. "No, I was wondering if you'd be willing to cater the desserts for it."

"Oh," Cash answered with a nod. "Of course. Please, come to my office, and we'll discuss details."

Things were already busy, and they'd only just started. Cash felt his heart beating fast. The future was bright... as long as nothing derailed it, of course.

Chapter 2

It had been a week since the reopening of the Fjord & Fika, and Cash finally felt as if he was settling in. So far, there hadn't been completely terrible incidents; only the one minor issue where Amelia had given someone the wrong change. It had left her flustered for about half an hour, but she bounced back after that.

Between Selena and Brian, the front was managed efficiently. They took turns with opening and closing shifts, and kept an eye on inventory levels. Cash wanted to ensure their new rye bread sandwiches filled with smoked salmon, house pickled capers and onions were plentifully stacked. Of course these were in addition to the cabinets stacked with sandbakkels and other delicious patisserie classics. Every now and again, one of the staff would pop into the office to give Cash an update on how things were going. This included several reviews about how people had been worried about quality dipping, but praised the team for keeping it so high.

Cash busied himself with getting stock and doing research on ways he could build on Sigrid's legacy. He barely ever found time to relax, but somehow living like this was still far more relaxing than the city had ever been. Life was good and fairly easy despite all of the trials and errors, and he was hoping that it would stay that way.

"Okay, budget," Cash muttered to himself as he opened the spreadsheets on his laptop and scrolled down to where he had left off the previous day. He adjusted the seagull pen cup a bit in a moment of procrastination before sighing and doing his best to refocus on the numbers. They were already starting to blur together somewhat, and the day was still long.

He considered helping in the kitchen as he had done a few times, at least for an hour or two, but he was falling behind on administration. It was where his expertise lay since he'd been in finance for years, and he'd done much more complicated things when he worked in the city from morning until night. Maybe that was why this was so difficult to focus on. There was no challenge to it; it just felt like entering numbers with no risk at all.

As he lifted his hand to start typing, though, there was a knock at the door. Cash looked up to see Brian coming in with a stack of booklets in his hands, excitement in his eyes and a bit of flour dust on his apron.

Cash raised an eyebrow. "Paperwork? Don't we normally do that on computers these days?"

"Oh, no, this—" Brian paused, placing one of the booklets on Cash's desk. "They're newsletters. You know Pete Jr., right? The 'former' mayor's son?"

Cash picked the offered newsletter up and scanned the front page without paying too much attention. Something about the mayoral race, a small workshop in the library, and someone's cat having their twentieth birthday. There was an obituary on the third page, and a few bits about the island's history.

"Mmhmm," Cash said with a nod, looking back up at Brian.

"Anyway, he's been saying he wants to reopen the newspaper," Brian continued with a sparkle in his eye. "And he's starting with these. Asked if we could display them out front. I said I'd ask the boss."

Brian seemed particularly excited about this new development. Along with the others, he'd grasped at everything that could improve the patisserie.

Cash thought about it for a moment. He remembered Pete as PJ from back in the day. They hadn't spent a lot of time around each other, but from what he knew, Pete had a history of mischief and misdemeanors. There had been a few rumors later on, but Cash wasn't sure how many of those were true.

He had no idea how Pete's life turned out as an adult, aside from the minor crime Cash had found out about during his investigation, and, of course, the fact that Pete's father was the one who had murdered Sigrid. It seemed a little odd for him to want to return to the island, but maybe he had his reasons.

Still, a newsletter could be a fun addition to the front counter. It could show Cash's care for the community and create things to talk about for patrons. And, from what he knew, the longer people spent time in a restaurant, the more they'd eat.

"Looks like he's serious about it, too," Brian said when Cash had been silent for almost a full minute. "I went over it; the stories are pretty good."

Cash nodded. "I suppose we could give it a chance."

He had already wanted the Fjord & Fika to be a true pillar of the community. A place where coming together was celebrated. Having the community newsletter there could be a good thing. Cash would keep an eye out, of course. He wasn't entirely sure whether he could trust Pete to do a good job consistently, but he didn't think that giving him an opportunity would do too much harm either way.

"Great," Brian said, grabbing the stack and bouncing his way out of the office.

Cash was left with a single newsletter and the looming knowledge that he had to get back to the budget. He'd managed to make it halfway through the next month, and things were looking good. At this point, he was even considering giving each of the employees a small raise. To do that, however, he'd need a projection for the next six months, and creating that was starting to feel like pulling teeth.

At least now he had a minor excuse to procrastinate, thanks to the newsletter. Cash picked it up again curiously and leaned back precariously in his office chair. He tried to picture what Pete would look like now, but all he could see was PJ, a kid with a sand-colored mullet and braces. He had always been a bit awkward, long-limbed, and roughed up with scuff marks from his misadventures.

He did remember his dark eyes, always looking for trouble, and seeming like they were deeper than Pete himself was. He never took a single thing seriously and always acted like he had no direction in life.

It was strange to think that he'd come far enough to want to reopen the island newspaper. Cash knew his mom's side of the family had been the ones who ran it when they were kids, long before Pete's father became the mayor. It had closed down about a year before the last time Cash had visited, though he wasn't entirely sure *why.* Frankly, he'd never even thought to ask about it, but now he was a little curious.

On the front page, Cash read the headline about the mayoral election, and immediately, he was intrigued.

"TROUBLE BREWING IN MAYORAL ELECTION," it said, splayed right across the top of the page. The election process had barely started, and it already seemed as if the island's gossips were stirring up something. That in itself wasn't particularly surprising; Cash himself had already been on the wrong side of the rumor mill.

Granted, people hadn't known him back then, and he'd known what the whole situation looked like. If he hadn't known the truth, he would have thought that he was guilty of Sigrid's murder, too. Even if that wasn't the case, he was sure that they'd have found something about him to talk about.

There wasn't much to do on the island if you'd been there your whole life. Most people easily fell into the gossiping rabbit hole. Usually, minor scandals were the most interesting thing that could happen.

What *was* surprising to him was the target of the scandal. Usually, gossip would involve suspected affairs or accusations of petty thievery. This time, however, it was different.

Emma's picture was small, overshadowed by the thick wall of the article's text, but there she was, caught in the corner of the page. It was one taken years after Cash had last seen his friend, but before his return to the island. In the image, she was smiling brightly. It was one that Cash recognized from the brewery's website, one taken from their "about us" section. And now here it was, attached to what seemed to be a pretty big deal.

Cash knew that Susan was running for mayor, alongside Orin, who Cash knew little about aside from their quick discussion on the debate's dessert when they first met. He had been pleasant and charming at the time, the type of man who could easily pass for a career politician. Dark hair, hazel eyes, and a smile that could make anyone trust him; that was what Cash had been thinking at the very start of their meeting.

Now, it seemed like he also knew the strategies of a career politician fairly well. First things first, you had to make someone else look like the villain.

So, Cash thought as he let his eyes scan the article. *How has he been attempting to make Emma seem like a completely horrible person?*

He frowned as he went over the first few paragraphs. The accusations seemed to be that Emma was guilty of unethical business practices, particularly in how she had acquired the brewery in the first place.

"Now, most people are aware of how long my family has been friends with Emma and her parents," Orin was quoted in one paragraph. "And far be it from me to drag her through the mud, but I want the people of Salt Cliff to know that transparency is the very foundation of my mayoral campaign. Especially when people in power use that to further their friends' financial interests."

Something about Orin's words didn't sit quite right with Cash, but he couldn't really put his finger on it. It made sense that a mayoral candidate would want to show themselves as transparent, particularly given the insanity of the secret that the previous mayor had. Orin had clearly pinpointed this as something that would be important to the community, and it looked like he was willing to do anything to prove himself.

But Cash simply couldn't imagine Emma as someone who would be involved in something shady, especially when it came to her passion—the brewery itself. It was something she had chased for a long time, and worked hard to not only get, but to build to what it was now.

"According to some sources," the article went on, "Mrs. Bennett had bought the brewery for a paltry sum after manipulating the previous owner into agreement due to his personal financial situation. There have also been claims that Susan Hawthorne used her political power to subvert paperwork."

Cash frowned again. He hadn't been on the island when Emma had bought the brewery, and he had no idea about the actual processes behind it or what she'd paid for it. Still, something was mighty fishy here, and he wasn't sure what that was. The article claimed that Emma had used less than savory means to get what she wanted. After all, it had been her biggest dream to own that brewery one day.

Absolutely not, Cash thought, sure that Emma wouldn't have gone down that route.

Maybe it was possible that she'd done everything in her power to make sure that her dream would come true. Maybe she found ways to save money, but that didn't mean she cut corners or used her relationship with Orin's father to get a lowball deal. But there was no evidence aside from Orin's word, and Cash didn't believe that Emma was that kind of person in the first place.

No way, Cash thought to himself, grabbing a pen from the seagull to tap on the desk as he went over things in his head. *She wouldn't do something like that.*

He simply couldn't convince himself that he didn't know her well enough to be certain that she was a woman of integrity. Even when they were children, Emma had always stood up for the "little guy." She'd always been someone who stood for justice. It just didn't seem like she could be a conniving criminal behind the scenes. She wouldn't have put anyone else down just to get what she wanted.

Lucas wouldn't have married her if that had been the case—at least, that was what Cash believed.

At the same time, Orin's accusations were written down so confidently on the front page of the newsletter. The further Cash read, the more confused he felt. Orin insisted that there was proof of Emma's deception and Susan's involvement. That he could, without a doubt, show the entire town her true colors.

Cash shifted in his seat as he read through the rest of the article. Orin claimed that the documentation was extensive. That Emma had used her close ties to his father to ensure that she'd get the brewery, which had been meant for the family. That she'd somehow manipulated him into believing he'd had no other choice.

"This can't be true," Cash muttered to himself when he'd finished the last sentence. "It just can't."

He attempted to browse through the rest of the newsletter, but none of it was enough to distract from that front page. He found himself pondering every word he had read, like thinking hard enough would help him read through the lines and find the truth.

Emma had never really gone into how and why she had gotten the brewery, at least not in any kind of detail. Nobody else had ever mentioned a scandal surrounding it either. But Cash didn't think that anyone would make an accusation like that without any kind of basis whatsoever. Perhaps Orin had *some* kind of documentation that could look suspicious, but could be explained innocently.

Cash stared at the open budget spreadsheets in front of him, clutching the newsletter in one hand. He was supposed to get this done today, or at least a fair chunk of it. But he knew perfectly well that he wasn't going to be able to focus on it in the slightest.

"Hey." Amelia stood at the door suddenly, peeking around it with a frown on her face. "Did you see?"

She glanced at the newsletter in his hand. "Oh, you did. Well, I don't think she did it, just so you know. Some people do, though. I've heard the customers whispering."

With that, she hopped off again, and Cash found himself already getting up from behind his desk. He folded the newsletter and placed it in his pocket. He knew that the questions weren't going to stop popping up in his mind. He needed to find the answers.

For now, the budget could wait. He had people he needed to talk to.

Chapter 3

With his mind full of questions, Cash left the office and made his way to the kitchen, where Selena and Amelia were busy creating fresh batches of baked goods. Both, however, turned curiously when Cash entered. Selena seemed to be busy rolling out dough, with Amelia standing nearby the oven to keep an eye on whatever deliciousness was baking within it.

"I have a few errands to run," Cash announced, trying to do so with a pleasant expression. "Selena, you're in charge."

She nodded at him and returned to her work, as did Amelia. Cash left the patisserie through the back, heading right for the old SUV at the far end of the parking lot. He wrestled with the driver's side door for a moment and got in, shifting himself until he was relatively comfortable. He often had to fiddle with the seat, which seemed to jump itself in and out of position of its own accord. The SUV seemed to have its own personality; most likely that of a grumpy old man being awoken from a midday nap.

Right now, he needed a moment to get his head straight. For a moment, he stared out at the view, the expanse of woods and hills growing in the distance. It wasn't something you got used to; even locals still found themselves staring every now and again. Cash himself often went out to the viewing points deep in the hills to stand around and contemplate life. It was a far cry from the constant hurry of the city, where he'd barely ever even had a chance to catch his breath.

I regret missing so many years here, he found himself thinking. He remembered visiting his aunt, his visits growing far and few between. He could have decided to stay on Salt Cliff many times, but he'd always convinced himself that his ambitions were more important. That wasn't the case anymore.

What he wanted now wasn't entirely clear, at least when it came to the far future. For now, he was happy settling into the island life and building the patisserie back to its former glory.

I should get moving, Cash reminded himself before he fell too deeply into his thoughts.

It took a few tries before the SUV roared—or rather, chugged—to life, and Cash pulled out of the parking lot to the sound of gravel and an unhappy engine. He tried to decide where to go first. Perhaps the best plan was to try and get a hold of Emma before he went off snooping of his own accord.

Cash pulled off the road, the SUV's suspension barely taking the edge off the hop onto the sidewalk.

A quick dial later, Cash held his phone against his ear, listening to Emma's phone ringing. Eventually, the phone disconnected; no answer. Cash tried Lucas's phone and even the brewery itself. No answers from any of them. Obviously, they'd already read the newsletter. Maybe their phones had been ringing off the hook, and they simply couldn't deal with all of it at once.

It made sense, given that they probably hadn't expected the accusations to come so suddenly in the first place. Nobody had. They had been running the brewery for several years at this point, and never even mentioned any scandal in acquiring it. Maybe there had been some sort of argument back then, but it seemed odd that something like that would be brought up so much later.

Should I stop by? Cash wondered as he placed his phone in the cupholder of the driver's seat and pulled the SUV back into the road. It was possible that they'd closed the brewery for the day and that they were trying to think of a response. In that case, it might not be particularly helpful for Cash to head there and ask questions.

Then what else? he thought, automatically taking the next turn into town. The roads here were not as narrow as up in the hills, but with the SUV's size, they still required careful driving.

Given that the accusations were linked to documentation, the most likely person who would be able to find the answers was Kieran. Perhaps there was something in the library's archives. It seemed like a good place to start, anyway. Kieran was the type of person who loved knowledge, in any case, and he'd likely be happy to help out with something like this. Especially since Emma was his friend too. She deserved their support.

Cash drove further into town until he spotted Jamie's red food bus on one corner. It seemed fairly quiet, with only two pairs of customers seated on one end of the seating area.

Cash parked the SUV nearby and shot a text to Kieran to meet him for coffee while he approached the bus.

Jamie popped their head out of the door and greeted him with a wide grin.

"Good morning!" they said brightly, hopping down onto the ground. "Looking for a cuppa?"

Today, they were dressed in a colorful mesh of fabrics, combining bright green pants with a yellow t-shirt and orange bow tie complementing their red apron. They'd even changed the color of their hair to a vibrant purple. It was a pleasant ensemble, one that reflected Jamie's pure joy to be alive.

"Always," Cash answered as he took a seat nearby. "Kieran's going to be joining me, so make it two."

"Great." Jamie headed back into the bus to get started on the order, while Cash pulled the newsletter out of his pocket and smoothed it out on the table in front of him.

He stared at the front page, somewhat hoping that certain words or clues would jump out at him. But he wasn't really learning anything more than he already knew, which wasn't much in the first place.

If he could figure out whether Orin was doing this out of some deep-seated anger, building resentment, or merely for political reasons, that would help. But it wasn't obvious from the article. Cash would have to talk to people who knew him better. Cash never really met Orin's family, even when he had visited Sigrid as a child. They were people that he'd greeted in passing but never had any kind of in-depth discussion with.

Jamie came to the table with the two coffees just as Kieran arrived and took a seat across from Cash. Today, he'd exchanged his brown bandana for an olive green one and was sporting a new vest over his loose-fitting shirt. Normally, Cash would have complimented it, but his thoughts were far too busy today.

Around them, the birds were singing up in the trees, a light breeze was playing over the world, and the distant buzz of town hummed in the background. It was the perfect moment on a tropical island, but Cash felt anything but relaxed.

He was already riding a thin line of tension, anticipation settling starkly in his chest. He was pretty convinced that something fishy was going on, and it wasn't Emma who was the perpetrator. They had to be framing her somehow, whether it was Orin doing it or someone else.

"Hi," Kieran said as he shook two sugar sachets into his coffee. "Your message seemed pretty urgent. What's up?"

"Haven't you seen this?" Cash asked, raising one eyebrow as he pushed the newsletter across the table. "I would've thought the library would be the first place to get them."

"Oh, yes," Kieran nodded. "They were dropped off this morning, but I hadn't really looked yet. Had a little workshop going on. Is it any good?"

Cash tapped on the front page with one finger. "You tell me."

Kieran scanned the page, and his smile quickly turned into a frown. He pushed his coffee to one side and picked the newsletter up, holding it close to his face as he read in more detail. Cash waited tensely, slowly stirring his own cup to keep his hands busy. Jamie passed by the table closely and curiously, like they were wondering what was going on. But, ever the professional, they didn't ask. Instead, they moved to their other customers, likely pretending not to eavesdrop.

Finally, Kieran let out a long breath and put the newsletter back on the table. "Whoa, that's certainly something."

"Do you know anything about it?" Cash pushed, leaning forward. "What documents are they talking about?"

Now, Kieran was the one raising an eyebrow. "You're investigating?"

"Look," Cash sighed. "Emma is my friend. This has to be affecting her badly. I need to know the truth, and so does everyone else."

He hadn't really thought of it as an investigation; more of a busybody looking into gossip.

"I see," Kieran said with a slow nod. "You don't think she's capable of this kind of thing..."

"Not in the slightest." Cash was insistent. He wasn't just going to believe a single article making wild accusations. But a lot of people would, and it would hurt Emma's reputation. If she really hadn't done anything wrong, then he had to prove it to the entire island.

"Will you help me?" Cash continued.

Kieran chuckled slightly, then smiled. "Yeah, I suppose I will. At least no one is dead this time, huh?"

Cash returned Kieran's energy with a dry laugh. "Luckily. Hopefully, this will be easier to figure out, too. There has to be something somewhere that can clear it all up, right? If it's just documentation that's the problem, anyway."

"Should we talk to Pete about it?" Kieran wondered further with a tap at his chin. "He'll have to issue a retraction or something if the information is wrong, won't he?"

Cash stared at his coffee for a moment. With Sigrid's case, the gossip had been bad, but there hadn't been much official press aside from online. He wasn't sure, however, that involving the physical press now was a good idea. Especially when Cash hadn't really met Pete in person since he'd come back, and he didn't know what kinds of stories he'd go for. Sensationalism wasn't going to help prove Emma's innocence.

He was a bit worried that it was only Orin's side that was being told. Cash didn't know much about journalism, but he found it strange that she hadn't gotten to say anything in her defense.

"Only once we have the whole story straight," Cash finally answered, taking a sip and noticing that his coffee was starting to really cool down.

With Sigrid's murder, Cash had gotten as many friends in on the investigation as he could have. This time, even without a murder, he was going to be more careful. He didn't want anyone else to fall in front of the wheels of scandal unnecessarily. He wasn't sure how people would react or whose side they would take. He needed more information.

"Fair," Kieran said thoughtfully. "But perhaps there are *some* people who could be particularly helpful."

Cash nodded, finishing the last of his coffee before speaking again. "Let's just talk to the most important people first. The ones we know are involved. Emma and Orin."

He had no idea whether Orin was the true source of the allegations or if he'd gotten his information from someone else. And, if he had, what were their intentions behind it? Orin's own were obvious; he wanted the position of mayor. But if someone else was pulling the strings, then there was something bigger going on.

"Mm, so we're splitting up?" Kieran asked. The more he spoke, the brighter the sparkle in his eye became. Whether he said it aloud or not, it was clear that he was excited about the whole situation. Not really about Emma being in trouble, but about the chance to investigate something again.

Before Cash could answer, Jamie appeared beside their table. "Please tell me you two are hungry. I've perfected my zaatar bagel. Fried egg and pomegranate with it. It's on special."

Cash and Kieran shared a glance.

On the one hand, Cash really wanted to get moving. On the other, he hadn't had breakfast, and his stomach was growling.

"I suppose we're going to need all the energy we can get," he finally said, and Jamie clapped their hands together.

"Perfect!" they exclaimed and disappeared into the bus' kitchen area to get the food ready.

Kieran and Cash sat in silent contemplation for a few moments. Cash ran through all of the questions he had for Emma in his mind. He didn't want to bother or overwhelm her, but he did want her to know that he was on her side and that he wasn't going to let this be swept under the rug.

"I'll talk to Orin," Kieran finally said with a firm nod. "I think Emma will be more willing to talk to you, anyway."

"Yeah," Cash agreed, fiddling with the cutlery on the table. "She might clam up, though."

"Well, you're not going to give up if she does, are you?" Kieran asked, amused. "I'm pretty sure you'll find your answers anyway."

Cash offered a sly smile in return. "Probably."

He was pretty sure that Emma would tell him *something.* Hopefully, she'd tell him more than enough for this investigation to be fairly easy. He wondered how far back this went. How long had she had a strained relationship with Orin? How many people knew about it? Where did it come from?

Cash knew he'd have to prioritize some questions over others. He didn't want Emma to feel like he was interrogating her.

Cups clinked as Jamie came to clear the table and placed a glass of water in front of Cash. He hadn't asked for it, but Jamie knew that it was something he'd want whenever he was going to eat something, given that he'd become a regular since he'd been on the island.

He took a big gulp, realizing that he was fairly thirsty. Kieran laughed. "Nervous?"

"Just haven't hydrated enough today," Cash answered before finishing the glass entirely. "Don't think I've quite gotten used to the weather here yet."

The conversation from there changed course, covering small talk and day-to-day pleasantries. Cash was already thinking about the next steps in the investigation, of course, but the deliciousness of Jamie's food was a fairly decent distraction.

Once they finished their meals and paid, Cash pushed his chair back and got up. Kieran did the same and followed Cash back to his SUV.

"Right, to confirm," Kieran said as Cash turned to him. "I'm talking to Orin, and you're going to see Emma. We'll reconvene afterward, right?"

"Absolutely," Cash agreed. "Keep your phone close. Let me know if you learn anything particularly important."

"Sure," Kieran answered, lifting a hand to shake Cash's before he walked away. Cash watched him leave, glad to have a good friend around whom he could trust. It was definitely easier than doing everything by himself.

Cash turned and got into the SUV, taking a few deep breaths and running over his questions in his mind before attempting to start it. It took several tries, but the SUV finally obeyed, and Cash pulled out onto the road. The streets were getting busier now, and Cash could imagine the whispers washing over them. There wasn't a lot of time to reverse all of this. If he didn't prove Emma's innocence soon, the image of her as a fraud could solidify in the community's minds.

Chapter 4

Cash noticed a few clouds starting to make their way across the sky in the distance, dotting the bright blue in shades of white and gray. There were more cars on the road now, too; mostly tourists in hired vehicles on their way to the beach. It slowed down Cash's progress somewhat, but also gave him a few moments to mull things over and get his questions straight.

Rain started dripping even while the sun was shining, a sign that a cloud break might happen soon. Cash imagined that some of the tourists would be disappointed in that, but to him, it was some of the coziest weather that the island had to offer.

When he pulled onto the brewery's road, he noticed that something was already going on up there. There were more cars than usual in the parking lot up ahead, and a whole crowd of people near the entrance.

Well, that's not great, Cash thought as he found a spot to squeeze the SUV into. It felt like the entire town's locals were gathering at the brewery to either find out more gossip or to possibly grill Emma about her alleged crimes. Whatever the case was, Orin's campaign strategy was obviously working. This kind of thing could easily split the whole town in two.

That wasn't good. The community had already been thrown into the deep end with the previous mayor's crimes. On top of that, they'd been split on the environmental impact of new developments, and the tourism that something like that could bring. The harmony that was usually among the people of Salt Cliff was tenuous at best at the moment. More arguments and issues could make that so much worse.

Cash shut off the SUV and got out with a deep sigh, wondering if he wasn't simply going to add to the chaos. Hopefully, Emma would see that he was there to help.

Gravel crunched beneath Cash's feet as he approached the crowd. It seemed like the brewery's front gate was closed, which wasn't surprising.

Around him, Cash could hear some of the whispers and speculations, while people at the front of the crowd tried to peer through the gate like they could see answers beyond the bars. There were at least two dozen people standing around, some Cash had seen around the island and some that he didn't recognize. All of them looked more curious than angry, but it could escalate easily if something went wrong.

He couldn't blame Lucas and Emma for shutting the place down, at least for a short while.

"Orin wouldn't lie," someone was murmuring to a friend. "Honestly, I've always thought there was something off about her."

"Me, too," another answered. "She's just... *too* nice, you know?"

"I *knew* she had skeletons in her closet," someone else said in what was likely supposed to be a hushed whisper, but came out far louder. "Nobody's *that* perfect."

"This generation, I'm telling you." An older, more shaky voice, sounding particularly annoyed. The man seemed familiar—Cash thought the man was named something like George or Geoffrey. Something with a G. He couldn't really remember.

Cash pushed past the crowd, trying not to let any of it get to his head. He weaved through until he was standing right up against the gate, the throng of bodies around him almost overwhelming. The humidity and the heat of the day weren't helping, either. On top of that, the drizzle of rain was starting to grow, with larger droplets and more intensity.

That didn't seem to bother the crowd. A few people had popped out their umbrellas already, and others were following suit. But nobody stepped away from the gates. Satiating their curiosity was clearly more important than staying dry.

Through the gate, Cash could see Lucas, standing near the bar, running a hand through his hair in frustration. He turned slightly and seemed to spot Cash from the corner of his eye.

Lucas dipped his head in the direction of the back of the brewery, and Cash nodded, immediately understanding.

Opening the front gate wasn't the smartest idea, even if it was just a smidge to let Cash in. He'd have to use the other entrance, one usually reserved for deliveries. Cash hoped that nobody would notice or follow him.

Soon enough, he was sneaking around to the back of the brewery, feeling a bit like a criminal. Luckily, none of the people at the front thought to do the same.

That was possibly because even with just a bit of rain, the route to the back was fairly muddy already. Cash felt his shoes sinking into the ground, and felt the mild annoyance as some of it managed to reach his socks.

Walking around all day with soggy feet wasn't going to be pleasant.

Lucas met Cash at the back and hurried him inside. He was led through to the back of the bar, where Emma was sitting, facing away from the entrance. Here, they were under a roof, but still able to hear and see the rain. Cash hoped that the rain would turn the world gray enough that the people beyond the gate would simply disappear into the mist.

Emma held her head in her hands, her shoulders shaking slightly as if she were crying. Her sobs, however, disappeared with the sounds of the people outside and the rain slowly increasing in its intensity. Lucas had been quiet until this point, as if he wasn't quite sure what to say. Cash had thought he'd run the two of them over with questions, but now it was as if he had forgotten his entire vocabulary.

What was there, really, that he could ask, without sounding like he was accusing Emma as well? If he jumped right into interrogation, she might take that as a lack of compassion from someone she considered a friend.

Eventually, Cash decided that he needed them to start talking first.

He took a seat near Emma and simply waited, hoping that she'd open the conversation at some point. Lucas stood beside her awkwardly, placing one hand on her shoulder for some sort of comfort. Cash glanced over his shoulder. From here, he couldn't really see the entrance. This section of the bar was blocked by signs, plants, and decor, but he could still hear the murmuring hum of people talking, and a few shouts as people called out to Emma to face the music.

"I didn't do anything," she finally muttered, lifting her face from her hands to face Cash. "I swear, Cash, none of it is true."

Her eyes were puffy and red, and her usually purposely tousled hair seemed messy. Even her flowing dress had more wrinkles than normal, as if it had the very life drained from it. It was pretty obvious that this tactic from Orin had affected her heavily. Cash shifted in his seat before he answered, leaning forward and offering her a sympathetic smile.

"I believe you," he said firmly. "That's why I came. Do... Do you think you can talk to me, or should I give you some time?"

"No, no, I'll be fine," Emma insisted, straightening herself up and fixing up her hair with a deep breath. "The quicker we do this, the quicker it can all be over, right?"

"I'll get us something to drink," Lucas said. He gave Emma's shoulder a quick squeeze before he left for the kitchen with stiff shoulders and a tight jaw. He seemed somewhat stoic, but Cash noticed the subtle signs that he was, possibly, even more worried about all of this than Emma herself.

"I assume you read the whole article, right?" Emma asked, and Cash nodded in return. "I can't believe Orin would twist the whole thing like this. I mean, I knew that he was upset about the sale, but... I didn't think he'd take it this far."

"Okay." Cash leaned on the bar with one elbow. "Can I ask you what actually happened? I mean, his father did own the brewery and eventually passed away, right?"

"He did," Emma replied with a curt nod. "But he sold it to me before that, a few months before, actually. And it was all legit, too. I didn't do something dodgy or fudge any papers or anything like that."

Lucas returned with three fresh glasses of juice and handed one each to Cash and Emma. Afterward, he simply stood next to his wife, wearing a frown and staring in the direction of the gate. His frustration was obvious, as was the fact that he felt somewhat helpless in this situation. Normally, Cash would have expected a smile and a joke from him, but it was clear that he saw absolutely no humor in this situation.

In fact, it looked a bit like he was ready to give Orin a piece of his mind, but was fighting not to run out and do so. Cash admired his attempt at stoicism, given how protective he was of Emma.

"So how did it actually happen?" Cash asked, choosing his words as carefully as possible. He didn't want Emma to think that he was throwing out any kind of accusation or that he doubted her. To figure out the truth here, whatever it was, she needed to trust him. So far, he was sure that she did, but she was in a precarious situation, and she might think that Orin's words had gotten to him.

"Well, Arthur—Orin's dad—he had gotten ill, and the medical bills were piling up," Emma explained, wringing her hands together. "He didn't really talk about that with his family as far as I'm aware. He didn't want them to worry. That's what he told me. I'm not sure if there was a different reason behind it."

Cash nodded along slowly, not wanting to interrupt Emma's thoughts. In his mind, he made his own notes, pinpointing places where he might have had more questions.

"I used to visit him all the time, because he was close to my parents," Emma continued tearfully. Her voice was shaking at this point, and it was clear that she was struggling to keep talking through her emotions. "And I overheard him talking to them about the illness. He was getting worse, and he knew that... Well. He knew it was going to be terminal."

Emma took a big breath. Cash took the moment to take a sip of his juice. The article had explained that their families were close. But from what Emma was saying, it seemed like her parents knew more of Arthur's troubles than his own child did.

That could certainly explain some of the resentment, especially if Emma had found out before Orin did, but it didn't mean that she'd done anything wrong. Nor did it mean that any of this was actually her fault.

"I thought he'd told his family," Emma finally said, placing her own juice beside her on the counter. "I mean, he eventually did tell them that he was sick, but not about the financial problems that it had caused. At least, that's the story as I know it."

She clasped her hands in her lap and looked down. "He knew that I wanted to own the brewery one day, so he called me and asked to talk. He explained everything and told me how much he needed to cover his debts and his funeral and stuff. And I wanted to pay more, but he wouldn't take it."

"Then you made the deal, right? On paper?" Cash asked, unable to stop the question from tumbling from his lips.

"Of course, it was on paper," Emma insisted, her cheeks flushed. "Everything was legal. I had lawyers involved and so did he. He was lucid and knew what he was doing. It was a long process, but I made sure that everything was done by the book. Orin was angry when he found out, but I wasn't there for the fights, just heard about them from my parents."

Cash nodded as he sipped at his juice. A family feud over inheritance. It was something he hadn't truly had to deal with when it came to Sigrid, at least not to an extreme extent. But he could appreciate that, in another context, it could be a bitter ordeal. It was unfortunate that Emma's dreams had to be entangled in something like that.

Still, being upset over losing the brewery couldn't be *all* that Orin had. Certainly, he wouldn't use that as a basis for his accusations.

"What about Susan?" Cash pushed further, wondering what the truth was behind her involvement. Orin probably didn't pull that out of thin air.

"She helped fill out the paperwork to transfer the business license, but that's all," Emma said, her eyes filled with fire. "Hardly any kind of *collusion.*"

"You still have all those documents, right?" Cash asked, and Emma nodded fervently.

"The copies are all at home. Arthur kept the originals," she said. "But maybe Orin has something else that will make people believe him over me... I mean... what do I do? Should I close the brewery?"

"No," Cash answered firmly. "That'll show him that you're rattled, and it'll just make the whole thing worse.

People will only be more suspicious. Keep the place open. Keep going like you always have."

"But I can't just ignore it all, can I?" Emma got up from her seat and leaned against the bar. "I have to do something. But *what?* Where do I even start?"

"Listen," Cash said, reaching out to grab Emma's wrist so that she looked him in the eye. "You know I believe you, right?"

"Yes."

"Well, then you should know that I won't rest until we've cleared your name," Cash went on, glancing at Lucas, who gave him an encouraging nod. "Lucas, can you find those documents?"

"Sure," Lucas said, his voice tight, but with some hope hidden within it.

"Seriously, Emma, don't worry too much about it," Cash continued as he let go of her wrist. "I will find the truth, and we'll show it to everyone. You're going to be alright."

"Thank you," she muttered with one last small sob. "Really."

Cash finished the last of his juice and left the brewery with a stormy mind. He'd gotten some answers, but a whole host of additional questions, too. How much had Arthur actually hidden from his family? What had been said in those arguments? What had been the original reaction when Emma first bought the brewery? Why bring it all up again now?

Cash walked with a frown as he thought, heading back to the SUV.

"Oh, sorry," Cash said when he suddenly bumped into someone walking his way. When he looked up, a guy offered him a flyer.

"Come 'round Tuesday," the guy said, not acknowledging Cash's apology. "Orin will tell everyone what really happened before Emma gets to twist the story."

The guy moved on, and Cash turned his eyes down to the flyer. It had the words "Community Transparency Meeting" plastered across the bottom. Clearly, Orin was already bringing the big guns, and he wasn't going to back off easily.

Cash had to move fast, before this whole situation spun out of control.

Chapter 5

With a shake of his head, Cash placed the flyer in his pocket, deciding that he'd go over it in detail later. Beside it, his phone started buzzing, and Cash pulled it out to check.

Are you getting the potatoes for the lefse? A text from Selena, a reminder of something Cash had completely forgotten about with his head in the clouds. He actually *did* have errands to run for the patisserie, one of which was collecting supplies. Mostly, he needed to get potatoes, since lefse was a dish that required a lot of them, especially if you wanted to cater an entire event.

Lefse had been one of the first choices that Cash had thought of. He remembered when he was younger, Sigrid often made several batches to freeze and keep for company. It was just as good that way as it was fresh. Cash hadn't had any in years, but he could still remember the taste.

Cash sighed, somewhat annoyed at the fact that he had real responsibilities outside of his investigation. He walked to the SUV and got it running before starting the drive down to the marina to grab the supplies he was supposed to get. Several things would have come on the supply barge, particular ingredients from particular sources that Sigrid, in her wisdom, had apparently always insisted on using. In fact, the potatoes themselves came from a specific set of farms on the mainland, which Cash didn't have any trouble finding thanks to Sigrid's detailed record-keeping.

The town itself was busy that morning, with tourists mulling about and locals taking advantage of the good weather. Cash parked the SUV close enough to the ferry terminal to make loading fairly easy, and then thought of Kieran, who had gone off to talk to Orin.

From what Cash did know, Orin owned the fishing shack near the marina, a long-standing local go-to for seafood. Cash hadn't been there before himself, but he knew more or less where it was.

Checking the time on his watch, he realized there was still about half an hour before the ferry carrying the goods would be in; enough time to check in on Kieran and ask a few of his own questions to Orin.

He got out of the SUV, the salty air immediately swallowing him. There was a slight breeze coming in from the ocean, and despite the clouds slowly drifting in indicating rain coming later that day, the air was fresh and cool. Cash headed down to the fish shack, watching the tourists around him enjoying their holidays and a few gruff locals working their way through the throng of people.

The shack sat on the edge of the beach, with an old surfboard as a name sign and a few fence posts driven into the sand as a border. Its walls outside were painted a dark blue, faded in some places and rusted away in others. It wasn't huge, but it had a strong presence.

Inside, fish and seafood filled various fridges and freezers, and the air smelled strongly of them. The lighting was brighter than Cash had expected. At the far end of the shack was a counter, behind which stood a brightly smiling cashier with dark hair. Kieran stood on the other side, talking to her. Their conversation sounded friendly and upbeat, though Cash couldn't quite hear the words above the buzzing of the fridges and the fans overhead.

"Hi! Welcome to the Salty Hook!" the cashier exclaimed brightly as Cash approached, and Kieran turned at the greeting. "I'm Pam, and I'll be your helper today. What can I do for you?"

"Hey! Haven't seen you in like, three days!" Kieran greeted, the minor lie coming across fairly naturally. "Pam and I have just been talking about you."

"Oh, so you're Mr. Kristiansen?" Pam laughed, offering him a sly grin. "Kieran says you're not happy with ol' Orin's little scandal."

Cash raised an eyebrow and glanced at Kieran, who simply shrugged. Pam waved them both off before she continued. "Nothing to worry about. Honestly, he's not the greatest boss. Bit of a grump, if you ask me. Though his customers would never know that, of course. Likes to smile when the public is around."

"Pam says that he's been looking more unhappy than usual lately," Kieran pointed out, clearly trying to steer the conversation in a particular direction.

"Really?" Cash asked curiously, and Pam nodded, probably eager to take this opportunity to gossip about her boss.

"Oh, absolutely," she insisted, wiping a stray hair behind her ear. "You'd think he'd be happy, being in the race and all. But I think someone told him Susan was pulling ahead, and she's friends with Emma, right? So, like, I think he wanted to smear her. I mean, everyone thought the business with the brewery was settled years ago."

"So there had been a problem with it before?" Cash questioned, trying to see how far he could push this.

"Yeah," Pam said. Her eyes were glittering with the excitement of someone getting to share premium gossip. "Orin's always been upset about it. He didn't want his dad to sell, and he fought tooth and nail to get the brewery back when Emma bought it. But he couldn't, and he said that the town was corrupt and conspired against him."

Cash listened closely. Clearly, Orin had been sitting on this for a long time, and he'd chosen right now to make his allegations for a reason. He had nothing on Susan, so he had to go for the people around her. Emma was the ideal target.

"Anyway, he says he can prove that his father's last will was forged, and that there were inconsistencies in

Emma's documents," Pam continued with wide eyes. "So, like—"

Pam was interrupted by another customer entering the shack. "Oh, a busy day. Hello, welcome to the Salty Hook!"

The woman who had entered nodded at Pam and smiled. "Having a look around, if you don't mind."

"Of course," Pam said, then turned back to Cash and Kieran. "Anyway, Orin says that Emma doesn't really own the brewery. Or, I mean, she *does,* but her documents aren't properly done, so the transaction shouldn't really have counted."

Cash noticed how the newest customer was slowly sauntering closer, as if she were just as curious about the juicy information that Pam was sharing as Cash and Kieran were.

"I see." Kieran tapped at his chin. "Has he been more specific about *how* the documents are problematic?"

"Ah, no," Pam sighed, as if this was some great disappointment. "But I'm sure he'll show it somehow. Maybe he's keeping it as a trump card. But, that's all I know, really."

"Right." Kieran nodded before he pulled out his phone, unlocked it, and handed it to Pam. "Why don't you give me your number, and you can text me if you hear anything else?"

Pam's eyes lit up. Cash wondered if she thought Kieran was making a move on her. Maybe he was, but Cash was fairly certain he was only after knowledge. In any case, Pam entered her number and handed the phone back.

"We should get going, anyway," Cash said to Kieran, knowing that they'd probably not get much more information, and he gave Pam a little wave. The two of them left the shack and stood on the beach outside, facing the ocean so that nobody could hear them.

"Do you think there are copies of those documents in the library?" Cash asked, drawing a line in the sand with his one foot as he thought through the dribs and drabs of new information they'd gotten. "The title papers and the bill of sale and... I mean whatever else could be related?"

"It's possible," Kieran replied, crossing his arms. "But I can't be entirely sure. Some of it might be in Town Hall instead. Still, could be worth a look."

"Will you?"

"You can count on me." Kieran turned to leave. "I'll text you if I find anything."

With that, Kieran walked away, and Cash headed in the direction of the ferry with even more questions. At least now they knew a little bit more, enough to expand their search but nowhere near what they needed to prove that Emma hadn't done anything wrong. It was still possible that Orin was bluffing, and that he didn't really have the evidence that he said he did.

But if that was the case, then why was he going to these lengths? Was he trying to hide something else by making this the focus of the news cycle? Why would he need to distract people if he didn't have any secrets of his own?

The ferry came in, and Cash got to work loading the crates of potatoes. It was monotonous labor, but that was a good thing, given that he had so much to think about. There were a few investigative avenues to go down with this whole thing, and it was possible that some information would only be available through official channels. Cash didn't want to get Town Hall involved, but it was possible that he didn't have a choice.

"Big dinner tonight?" The familiar voice made Cash look up.

Sheriff Riley Thompson stood a few feet away, his wide shoulders and stubble creating a bit of a fluttering in Cash's stomach.

He smiled awkwardly at Riley and scratched the back of his neck. "Supplies, actually. Uhm, you know, for the patisserie."

"Mm, I haven't been in a while," Riley mused, taking a step forward and picking up one of the crates. "I should grab a few pastries sometime."

"Whatever you'd like," Cash answered, immediately feeling a bit stupid. He quickly cleared his throat and picked up a crate. "I mean, we're still using Sigrid's recipes and everything."

"As long as you're keeping busy and not playing private investigator." There was a teasing tone in Riley's voice. Cash's eyes widened for a moment as he realized this, and it made him feel like he wanted to giggle. But he held back.

"I have responsibilities," he said instead, staying as vague as possible. Nothing he was investigating right now was particularly dangerous, anyway. It wasn't illegal, and he wasn't getting in Riley's way. Therefore, Riley didn't need to know.

"Mmhmm," Riley murmured, sounding like he didn't really believe Cash. But he didn't question him. "So, you bake it all yourself, then?"

"I mean, I have employees," Cash laughed as they reached the SUV, placing the crates inside, before going back for the last pair. "I don't do *everything* myself."

"Pretty sure you could," Riley replied, glancing at Cash with a look in his eyes that made Cash's cheeks heat up. "After all, you did catch a murderer."

"Didn't do that alone, either," Cash pointed out, bending to pick up the second-to-last crate, while Riley took the other. "Frankly, doing things alone usually isn't a lot of fun, anyway."

"Well, then maybe we should do some things less alone, uh..." Riley paused halfway through his sentence, as if he wasn't sure how to finish it. "I mean, you know, like... More community stuff."

Cash wasn't sure what to answer. Some part of him thought that Riley was attempting to ask him on a date, while another argued it was just the sheriff being friendly. Either way, it was unexpected. Quietly, Cash and Riley placed the last of the crates inside the SUV before they faced one another again.

"Thank you," Cash finally said, adding a smile that seemed anything but natural.

I'm really terrible at this, he found himself thinking, hoping that his awkwardness wasn't showing on his face.

Riley cleared his throat and reached out to shake Cash's hand. "I should get back to work."

Cash took Riley's hand, shook it, and the two of them held on for a second too long before they let go—slowly and uncertainly.

"Uh, anyway, yeah," Riley said, nodding several times and starting to whistle as he walked away.

Cash watched him leave with a still-fluttering stomach and a pretty strong sense of confusion about the whole thing. He wasn't entirely sure whether he was just seeing things or if there really was some sort of chemistry between the two of them.

Right, I'm going to grab lunch, Cash thought, locking the SUV and turning back toward the marina. There were a few places where he could get a good snack, and he needed a few minutes to get his head straight.

"Mr. Kristiansen, right?"

Cash looked up from his feet at the sound of his surname. He was faced by a guy with a familiar face, though far older than Cash remembered. He had sandy blond hair and a cheeky moustache, dark eyes dancing with mischief, and tattoos peeking out from behind the sleeves of his leather jacket.

"Pete?" Cash said curiously, surprised at how handsome the ex-mayor's son had become in adulthood.

"So you *do* still have that lightning-quick memory, then," Pete answered with a grin, crossing his arms comfortably. "You grew up well."

Pete let his eyes scan Cash's body, and Cash immediately felt his heart skip a beat. Pete was clearly charming; effortlessly so. But Cash had to be careful here. Pete probably knew that Cash and Emma were still friends. Perhaps his charm was simply a ploy to get more information about her for his newsletter.

"So did you," Cash replied confidently.

"Ah, it's been quite a road," Pete laughed, an effortless sound that probably made him the life of any party. "You know, I wasn't going to come back. I mean, I did, for my dad..." Pete trailed off before he shook his head.

"But that's over now, right? He did what he did, and he deserves to be in jail forever. I'm uh... I'm sorry, for what it's worth."

Cash wasn't sure what to answer to that. It wasn't Pete's fault that his father was a murderer, but it certainly did make things a little bit more awkward. Pete seemed to recover quickly, however, moving on to his next topic with surprising smoothness.

"Thanks for letting me put out the newsletters at your place, by the way. Really helps. What do you think about them?"

Cash paused for a moment, then nodded. "Well, honestly, I think the town might have enough gossip as it is."

To his surprise, Pete chuckled in reply. "Exactly why we need a trustworthy news source, don't you think?"

"Ah, fair enough," Cash said, though he wondered inwardly if Pete's newsletter, or rather, the paper he was trying to get off the ground, actually would be trustworthy at all. With Orin's accusations, the article itself seemed neutral enough, but the quotes were clearly sensationalist.

Maybe that wasn't what Pete intended entirely, or maybe he simply wanted to have a big start to keep the newsletter going. Either way, Cash wasn't going to trust him right away, even if he was particularly handsome.

"Right, I have a story to get to," Pete announced, patting Cash on the shoulder in a friendly way. "I'll talk to you again, yeah?"

"Sure," Cash said, walking in the opposite direction, back toward his SUV. He was still hungry, but perhaps lunch in the office would be better if he wanted space to actually think.

Chapter 6

It was now a few days later, and Cash found himself running around preparing for the mayoral event at the brewery to the point that he barely had any time to pay attention to his investigation. The whole thing constantly hung at the back of his mind, and he kept checking in with Kieran to see if there were any updates.

Until now, however, Kieran hadn't found much, apart from a few posts on social media from when Emma had bought the brewery that congratulated her. It was looking more and more like they'd have to involve Town Hall and go through the torture of bureaucracy to get their answers.

Cash had the newest newsletter in his hand and was flipping through it quickly to see if there had been any new news on Emma or Orin. But the only thing around the mayoral event was an announcement with information on the venue and times. Most of the rest of the newsletter simply covered a few local landmarks and their history, and there was an excellent review of Jamie's food truck.

With a sigh, Cash checked his watch. It was time to start getting ready for the event; those desserts weren't going to make themselves. Hopefully, after a deeply busy evening, he'd be able to get back to clearing Emma's name.

Cash got up from his office chair after putting the newsletter in one of the drawers; even if it wasn't entirely relevant, he still wanted as many close-enough documents as he could get.

Amelia and Selena were already in the kitchen, with Brian handling the front. Cash himself would be taking over some of Brian's share of the cooking, after some more practice sessions to get all of Sigrid's desserts *just* right. For now, most of his help in the kitchen consisted of assisting the others; Brian closely watched him whenever he actually did do some of the steps himself.

It was heart-warming that everyone at the patisserie took Sigrid's teachings so seriously, but also mildly inconvenient. Cash was impatient to really get cooking, but he knew that he had to make her proud.

"Okay, let's get started," Cash said as Amelia and Selena jokingly saluted him. "Are there enough premade items to keep front-of-house stocked until end of day?"

"Yeah," Amelia answered with a vigorous nod. "Unless we get seven lunch rushes in a row."

"Should be fine," Selena grumbled.

She'd been in a bit of a mood all day, but Cash hadn't pried. Selena simply sometimes had a case of the grumps, and he'd learned not to push. She was still fantastic with the customers and never put a foot wrong when it came to her work. Frankly, Cash was sure that he just needed to get used to her personality, and they'd grow nearly as close as she and Sigrid were.

It was also likely that she was still mourning Sigrid as much as he was. She'd been his aunt's longest employee and worked with her every day. Watching a master and then having to follow a novice must have been frustrating for her.

"Right, then Amelia, help me get the potatoes ready," Cash delegated. "And Selena, get mixing. We don't have a lot of time, and this is definitely going to take the longest of all."

They all jumped into action like a well-oiled machine. Selena went to gather cream, cardamom butter, salt, sugar, and flour, and prepare it all to be mixed into the potatoes later. Amelia and Cash were working on peeling the potatoes and throwing them into the vegetable sink to get washed.

It was a fun thing to be part of, something Cash could almost not imagine he had missed out on for so long. At some point, he even started whistling, and Amelia joined in on the song. Selena continued her part quietly, but she had never been the type for overzealous enthusiasm. Even so, he noticed her head moving slightly to the music, which made him think that she was ecstatic to be working on this.

"I'm always surprised at just how many potatoes lefse needs," Amelia pointed out about a third of the way through their peeling adventure. "It looks like we're planning to feed a small village."

Cash laughed and shook his head. "You should've seen me carrying all of them to the SUV. I'm turning into a bodybuilder."

Saying that made him think of Riley and the rugged smile on his face as they spoke to one another. A flutter went through Cash's stomach, and he had to clear his throat to stop himself from blushing in front of Amelia. Riley had an effect on Cash that he couldn't deny, but he wasn't sure that either of them were ready for an actual relationship.

Maybe Cash would ask Riley out one day, once he was properly settled and had worked through most of his grieving. For now, though, he had more important things to focus on than whirlwind romances and dreams of dating a sheriff.

"I like that Emma is still hosting the event," Amelia mused, seemingly oblivious to Cash's awkwardness. "She's not backing down, you know?"

Cash was proud of her for that, too. It was one step toward proving her innocence that she wasn't afraid to face the public. She was standing up for herself and holding her head high. It was a difficult thing to do. Hiding might have saved her from a lot of the scrutiny.

"Mm," Cash agreed, "because she hasn't done anything wrong."

He heard a slight noise from Selena's direction, but couldn't quite make it out. He looked over his shoulder and saw she was leaning against the counter. She had her arms crossed and the ingredients all laid out behind her. As Cash expected, they had been precisely measured and placed in the exact order that Sigrid had listed them in the recipe. It was clear why Sigrid had chosen to mentor her; they had a similar insistence on perfection when it came to food.

"Ingredients are ready," she announced with a small smile. "Do you mind if I help out Brian while I wait for the potatoes?"

"Sure, that'd be great," Cash answered, but his thoughts were already traveling back to Emma. He wasn't feeling particularly good about lagging behind on his investigations, and she'd been vague any time he'd checked in with her. She insisted that she was alright and that the curiosity of the islanders had somewhat died down.

But Cash wasn't so sure about that. Orin had had his rally just two days earlier, and with what Cash had been hearing from accidentally eavesdropping on customers, people's interest had definitely been renewed.

Plus, there hadn't been any other major scandals to distract them. Cash wasn't sure they'd stop talking about all of this for a while; unless there was another council meeting called about developments or the impact of tourists on the island environment. And as far as he knew, one wouldn't be scheduled for several more weeks.

"Uh, I don't think that's going to get peeled with that particular technique," Amelia said, pulling Cash back to reality. He looked down and realized that, while he was in thought, he had managed to turn the peeler around and was essentially rubbing a potato with the back of it. Clearly, his focus wasn't really where it was supposed to be.

He chuckled and corrected the peeler. "I mean, experimentation is always good, but maybe I'll put that one on the back burner."

"Sounds like a good idea," Amelia answered with a mock-serious nod. They continued peeling in silence, working in a synchronized rhythm that made Cash smile. Amelia had already learned a lot in the short time since he'd taken over the patisserie, and every day her confidence had been growing. If Sigrid had been there, she'd definitely have been proud of Amelia's progress.

"There!" she announced proudly once the last potato was dropped into the vegetable sink.

She began washing them while Cash prepared the army of pots that they needed to cook everything until soft. Luckily, they had more than enough stovetops to do so. Once the potatoes were ready, Cash and Amelia put them into the pots with some water, ensuring balance and even numbers in each one.

Cash had almost added a few pinches of salt to each pot, which if he had not been reading closely, was exactly as Sigrid had noted not to do in her in the margin of her recipe. “Never rush the potatoes.” It was one of the things that she'd never told her employees, but something she insisted in her notes made an enormous difference.

"Okay, I'll take over for now," Cash told Amelia. "Why don't you help out in front? I'll call you when I'm ready."

She nodded and left the kitchen with a bounce in her step.

In his mind, Cash followed along with the process, almost hearing Sigrid's voice as he did so. First, the pots needed to be brought to a boil. Then, the heat needed to be brought down to medium-low, and everything had to be left to simmer for the next twenty minutes.

Perfect timing, Cash told himself as he stood back from the stoves and smiled. *Sigrid would have been proud.*

That thought made him somewhat teary-eyed, and he took a deep breath to steady himself. He still wished that he had come to the island earlier. Even a few hours could have made an enormous difference. But now, it was too late, and all he could do was to make sure that Sigrid's legacy endured.

For now, he was still pretty impressed with his skills when it came to doing that. The business was afloat, his employees were happy, and the food was pretty great.

Cash glanced at the timer. Sixteen minutes left. He considered letting it be and getting a few other things done while he waited. At the same time, he was slightly worried that something unexpected would go terribly wrong if he even dared to take his eyes off the pots.

As he was thinking this, Selena came into the kitchen to grab something.

"Lunch rush," she announced, tucking a loose strand of hair behind her ear. "It's getting nice and busy in there. You need anything?"

Cash shook his head. "I've got it covered. I'll let you know when it's time for your section."

Selena nodded, though she did sneak a peek at the potatoes, probably to make sure that Cash was still doing everything absolutely perfectly. Then, she grabbed the jam she'd come for and rushed out of the door again.

Cash himself grabbed a nearby stool and took a seat, deciding that he'd simply let his thoughts wander for the rest of the time that the potatoes needed to get soft enough.

When the timer finally went off, it made Cash jump, and he hurried to get everything off the stoves. Within a minute, Amelia had appeared in the kitchen again, ready to help get the potatoes through the ricers and cool them off. It was a step that needed to happen quickly, given that the potatoes had to stay hot while going through the ricers. If they cooled off too much, it would all be ruined.

Well, not really, but Cash knew that things had to be perfect. "Okay" simply wasn't acceptable. This had to be a dish that would blow the minds of anyone who tried it. This was his first catering event since he'd taken over the patisserie, after all. Lefse was a simple dish, but he still had to make sure that it stood out.

"It's Selena's turn," Amelia pointed out once everything was on the counter, and Cash was monitoring the temperature. "I'll get her."

"No, I'll do it," Cash answered quickly. "I need a breath of fresh air, anyway. You check her tables."

"Alright!" Amelia squeaked and bounced off to the front. Cash followed at a far more leisurely pace, though still fast enough that the potatoes wouldn't cool too much before Selena could do her part.

She was standing at a table, serving a pair of regulars, when Cash waved her over.

"It's ricing time," he said and comically rubbed his hands together.

To his surprise, Selena let out a small chuckle and nodded.

"Sure," she answered as she passed.

Cash headed outside for a quick break. He found himself standing under a blue sky, the perfect weather for a mostly outdoor event. The parking lot was relatively full, but he could still hear the island's sounds beyond it.

Cash checked his phone. There was a text from Kieran. Still nothing about the documents they were looking for, but Emma had brought copies of hers to the library. That was good. They'd have something to search through at least.

In his mind, Cash went through his schedule for the next few days, doing his best to find a bit of time to put aside for the investigation. After the event, he was sure he could dive into it. He just had to make it through the evening.

After a few minutes of relaxing, Cash returned to the kitchen, where Selena was almost finished mixing all of the necessary ingredients into the still-hot potatoes. Normally, ricing would have taken a surprisingly long time, but Sigrid had invested in a fancy ricer attachment to support larger volumes faster.

Selena was so focused on what she was doing that she didn't even turn when Cash entered. That was a good thing, and probably the reason why Sigrid had always assigned the most complex parts of recipes to her.

"Almost ready for cooling?" Cash asked, peering past her at the bowls of potatoes. They were still warm but not steaming, just at the right temperature for the mixing. He could almost feel Sigrid nodding at him that they were doing a good job.

Selena peered over her shoulder, noticed him, and smiled. "Absolutely. These are going to be incredible, I'm telling you. Sheer perfection. Measured everything down to the gram."

"Wonderful," Cash said, starting to transition some of the bowls to the cooling rack to get them down to room temperature. From here, it would be Brian's turn, and he'd get the lefse to its final, crispy form. It would take at least fifteen minutes for things to cool down, though, and time was starting to crunch.

Cash checked his watch. They did still have a few hours, but there was a lot to get ready. He himself had to make a few calls, go check in with Emma and the brewery staff, prep the cutlery... There was a whole list.

But at least one thing was definitely taken care of. He knew that the lefse would be the star of the evening, something that would have people coming back for more. It was probably one of the best dishes he had helped make since he took over the patisserie, and would definitely be difficult to beat.

"Right, I have to get everything else in order," Cash told Selena, slightly sad that he wouldn't be there for the finishing flourish. "Do you have this covered?"

She turned to look at him with the last bowl of potatoes in her hands. "No worries, boss, it's going to be great."

Chapter 7

Several calls, checks, and bits of planning later, it was finally time to put everything in the SUV and get moving toward the brewery. Brian volunteered to stay behind to handle sales until closing time, while Selena and Amelia would join Cash in getting things ready at the venue itself.

"Let's get it all packed," Cash said as the three of them stood in the kitchen with the packaged desserts. "Hopefully, we'll have enough space."

"We'll squeeze in," Amelia said optimistically. "Don't you worry."

They got everything into the SUV, and with Selena in front and Amelia carefully arranged along with the boxes in the back, started heading out to the brewery. With the heavier load, Cash could feel every bump in the road, and it was making his jaw tighten. Everything was shaking, but he could see Amelia in the rearview mirror, holding on to the lefse and the lemon curd sandbakkels for dear life so that they wouldn't be damaged.

Cash slowed down as much as he could, hoping that everything would survive. Still, he believed in the SUV's ability to get things done, and they continued at a steady pace straight to the brewery.

He had faith that today wouldn't be the day that the SUV broke down, and breathed a sigh of relief when they finally pulled into the parking lot and came to a stop—with everything still intact. Someday, he'd probably have to replace it with a better vehicle, but for now, it was still doing its job well enough.

"We made it!" Amelia laughed as she tumbled out of the back seat and did a few stretches outside.

"That was stressful," Selena added as she got out and immediately started checking the desserts in the back.

The three of them gathered everything together and took it inside, although it took several trips. Finally, everything was stored in the kitchen and waiting to be eaten. There wasn't a lot of time before the event would officially start. People were already arriving at the front of the brewery, where Lucas was slowly letting them in.

When he was completely finished in the kitchen, Cash headed out to start mingling. If he was honest, he really wanted to listen in on the conversations that people were having.

He noticed Pete standing to one side, taking a few pictures and talking to people who were attending. Cash had to wonder if he was trying to get quotes to further stoke the pot with the scandal he believed he had uncovered.

Cash had thought he needed to focus on getting updates on the situation himself. To see how opinions had evolved on Emma and on the election. From what he'd heard in the patisserie, opinions were relatively split. He didn't think that they would have been if Orin hadn't gone after Emma so hard. Given that Emma and Susan were known to be well-acquainted with one another, it made sense. Especially if people believed that Emma had done something, and that Susan did not denounce those actions.

"Look, he's honest, and that's important." A sentence Cash caught from where he stood sipping on a long glass of complimentary orange juice. "Sure, he doesn't have a lot of experience, but isn't that what we want? Someone who isn't a career politician?"

"I don't know." The answer came from whoever had spoken's conversational partner. "Susan's done a lot for the town, and I mean, there's just *something* about him that puts me off."

These seemed to be general opinions, from one side and the other. Cash caught more people speculating on who would be a better leader; someone with experience and a proven track record, or a fresh face who wasn't afraid to speak his truth. Cash wondered if Orin had actually believed everything he said or was making things up just to get ahead in his campaign. Whatever the case was, Cash had to get to the bottom of it. Maybe he could get a moment at some point to talk to Orin himself, though he wasn't quite sure how he would phrase the questions he needed to ask.

Nobody was spending too much time talking about the accusations themselves, which was a relief to Cash. Still, he knew it would be important to Emma that her name was cleared completely, that nobody would have any reason to question her in the future. Beyond that, it was possible that Orin would push more "awareness" of the accusations if they seemed to die down, to keep people talking. The more he was at the front of their minds, the better for his campaign.

"Cash, hi." Upon hearing his name, Cash turned, for a moment expecting to be scolded for eavesdropping. He was faced with Susan, who was smiling and reaching out to shake his hand.

Cash hadn't spoken to Susan much after Sigrid's funeral, but she was always polite and relatively pleasant when he did. She was currently dressed in a neat gray pantsuit that went well with her silver hair and glasses, perfectly polished as usual. A pin reading "Vote Susan Hawthorne for Progress" sat on her lapel in gold, standing out against the rest of her outfit.

"Hi," Cash greeted and took her hand. "Nice to see you."

Susan glanced around at the still-growing crowd. "Full house. That's good. We need more people to take the town's politics seriously."

She didn't seem to have an ounce of anxiety over the coming debate. Cash himself had never been completely comfortable in front of a crowd, but Susan didn't have that same problem. He'd seen her speak before; it was a completely natural thing for her, as if she was born for public office.

Cash wasn't sure that all of the attendees were there for politics. It seemed like many were waiting for the next little bit of juicy gossip. It was more interesting than anything else happening on the island. Plus, this was the first time that Susan and Orin would face off with one another directly. Still, it was one way to get people more involved in what happened to the community.

"I suppose so," Cash answered. For a moment, an odd silence hung between the two of them. Susan's expression told him that there was something she wanted to tell him, but she was hesitant. Hesitation had never been something Cash experienced when it came to Susan. She was never afraid to speak her mind.

That made Cash curious. Susan had inherited a few of Sigrid's personal things, little trinkets that didn't mean much to Cash, but probably had significance for Susan. She hadn't mentioned anything about them before, and Cash hadn't thought she would. But it was the only thing he could think that she'd want to talk to him about. Or, maybe she wanted to ask if she had his vote, or even if he'd want to be more involved with the development campaigns.

Whatever it was, when she spoke, it seemed like she'd decided against telling him.

"I heard you made the desserts," Susan finally said, and Cash almost raised an eyebrow. She crossed her arms, as if she'd decided against telling him whatever it was that was truly on her mind.

"Well, I had help." Cash shrugged. "But, yes. Exactly according to Sigrid's recipes."

"Then I have a lot of faith in this event's catering," Susan firmly announced with a smile. "It will almost be as if she's still here..."

Her voice trailed off, her smile turning into something else—longing, maybe—but Cash couldn't be sure. Then, Susan shook her head and finally nodded at Cash.

"I should get ready. I'll talk to you again later."

Susan put her hand on Cash's shoulder for a moment, then walked away, leaving him still curious about what was on her mind. He made a mental note about it for later, filing it between the questions he still had about Orin's accusations.

The venue soon filled up, and the moderator, Morgan, took to the stage to announce that the debate between Orin and Susan would be starting soon. They offered everyone a smile and a warm welcome, and people began gathering around tables. Cash spotted Kieran at a distance, weaving through to join him closer to the bar counter.

"You chose a good spot," Kieran pointed out once he reached Cash. "Good view of everyone, far enough from the speakers not to be overwhelming, but close enough to hear well. Nice work."

Kieran was as relaxed as always, leaning back on the barstool he sat in with his shoulders low and his legs dangling comfortably off the edge. He had a personality far different from Cash's own, but that was one of the reasons that their friendship had grown so strong.

"I hadn't even thought of that," Cash said with a quick, dry laugh. "But I suppose you're right."

"I usually am." Kieran smiled. "Anyway, listen, I haven't found much in the archives yet. I mean, an article or two, some old ads for the brewery when the newspaper was still around. But nothing worth noting, no official documents or anything like that."

Cash nodded slowly. "So, either there wasn't a lot of news about it and it wasn't a scandal back then, or..."

"Or it was covered up somehow," Kieran ended the sentence. "Indeed. I'm not sure which. I'll keep looking. Maybe it was hidden somewhere in the back. Though if they really wanted to cover something up, it's possible that everything was destroyed."

"Perhaps," Cash agreed, taking a long sip from his drink before continuing. "But they wouldn't be able to destroy documents at Town Hall, would they? Maybe there's something there."

Cash noticed Brian coming in from the front gate, and he waved at him. Brian hurried over and leaned in to talk to Cash.

"Locked up and ready for the morning," he said. "Was pretty quiet after you left."

"Great, thanks."

"I'll go see what I can do in the kitchen."

When Brian walked away, Cash turned back to Kieran.

"Town Hall could be worth a look. Probably have to ask someone who works there," Kieran said as he adjusted himself on his stool. "Oh, looks like they're about to start."

The conversations in the brewery started dying down as Susan, Morgan, and Orin approached the stage and each took their positions. They adjusted their microphones and did a quick audio test while the audience's attention slowly drifted toward them until everything was almost entirely silent.

Both Susan and Orin were smiling at this point, and Morgan was the first to approach the microphone. They welcomed everyone to the event and reminded people to wait with questions until they opened the floor to them. Then, it was time for opening statements.

"As you all know," Susan began, standing tall with her shoulders squared. "I have dedicated my life to Salt Cliff Isle and its people. Today, I hope to show..."

She continued her speech with confidence and a perfect kind of practiced intonation. She was easy and pleasant to listen to, and it was clear that she was used to speaking in front of people.

Orin managed to keep up a similar level of energy and confidence, despite not being similarly skilled in public speaking—at least, given his occupation. Cash wondered if he'd had some kind of training at some point in his life, or if this was simply a result of his personality.

Soon enough, however, the debate left the zone of painted politeness and headed in a more hostile direction.

"Certainly, with your work, you must have been aware of the previous mayor's corruption in some way," Orin was saying at one point.

Somehow, Susan kept her tone and her face even when she answered.

"Unfortunately, he managed to keep his dealings hidden," she admitted, sounding somewhat somber. "But with the help of Sigrid Kristiansen's investigation and Town Hall's work, we were able to uncover it and take immediate action. Currently, corrective measures are being taken in impacted departments."

"Oh, how conveniently vague," Orin laughed and rolled his eyes.

"If you'd like to get into it, we can," Susan immediately answered.

"We don't have too much time," Morgan interrupted. "We should move to the next question."

By the end of the debate, the atmosphere was fairly heated, and the audience seemed split almost exactly halfway. However, it did look, to Cash at least, as if

Susan had a small advantage over Orin in terms of support.

Cash couldn't really stay and listen to everyone's opinions, however, since he had to head to the kitchen to get the desserts ready for serving. Brian, Selena, and Amelia were all already there, plating items and getting them to look nice. The main finger foods had been served throughout the debate, and the desserts would be the last "event" of the night.

There wasn't a lot of talking; just grabbing and carrying out into the brewery. Conversations overlapped one another, and Cash was so focused that he couldn't really hear many of them. However, he did notice the praises the desserts were receiving and smiled to himself.

"I have no idea what these are," one person commented about the lefse. "But I need twenty more of them."

Cash's heart skipped a beat as he thought of Sigrid and how proud she would be that he was doing this. She'd probably be impressed with the success of the recipe, though she might not have shown an extreme level of enthusiasm. Perhaps a simple wink and a "good job."

It took almost an hour for everyone to finish their desserts and to get things cleared out. Finally, attendees started to filter out through the front gates. When the last people had left, Cash, Amelia, Selena, Lucas, the brewery's server Jessica, and Emma were left behind to clean up.

With everyone being particularly tired, there wasn't a lot of chatting. Brian and Amelia cleared the tables while Selena removed table cloths, Jessica mopped the floor, and Cash, Emma, and Lucas started on the dishes in the kitchen. Cash took the time to let his thoughts wander, though he did throw a few glances in Emma's direction to try and gauge her mood. She seemed to be more focused on cleaning than anything else.

At some point, Selena came to grab the SUV's keys from Cash to get their equipment and cutlery back to the patisserie.

"I've gotten my documents together," Emma eventually said over her shoulder. "I'm pretty sure they'll prove everything on their own, but... Maybe not. Maybe people would think that I forged them somehow."

Cash paused halfway through drying a plate. "Kieran's still looking on his side. We'll find something, I know we will."

"Yeah," Lucas agreed, squeezing Emma's shoulder. "We all know that you're innocent. Orin's using you for his own politics. You don't have anything to worry about."

"I know, it's just—"

Emma's sentence was interrupted by a bloodcurdling scream that made all three of them freeze. It was as if the entire world had become silent, swallowed by that one sound. It felt as if an eternity had passed before Jessica burst into the kitchen, out of breath, wide-eyed, and completely pale.

"There's..." she started, before swallowing, taking a few shallow breaths, and trying again. "There's a body in the dining room!"

Chapter 8

For a moment, nobody reacted, as if all of their minds were struggling to process what they had just been told. Cash wasn't actually sure that he'd heard Jessica correctly. But she didn't look like she could repeat it. At this point, she was hyperventilating and she had tears in her eyes.

She shook her hands wildly and shifted from one foot to the other, as if her panic had nowhere to go. Still, nobody moved; like she could tell them that this was a joke at any point. But she didn't.

Finally, Emma stepped forward and grabbed Jessica's arm. "Are you sure?"

Jessica, shaking, nodded. Emma looked back at Cash and Lucas. "Maybe you should check?"

Cash did not want to do any such thing. There were already flashes in his mind of the day that he'd found

Sigrid. It was not an experience that he wanted to repeat. At the same time, someone had to do it, and he didn't want Lucas to go alone.

"Okay, stay here," Cash said, glancing at Jessica one last time. "Just... Breathe."

Lucas was the first to start moving, and Cash followed. Having heard the commotion, Brian and Amelia walked after them, too, both curiously and cautiously. Emma stayed with Jessica in the kitchen, trying to calm her down.

Cash felt his muscles tighten the closer they got to the dining room. It was an area that had mostly remained closed, given that Lucas had been busy renovating it the last few weeks. It was supposed to be a new feature for the brewery, a place for smaller, more intimate events. But if Jessica was right, then, well, Cash wasn't sure what that would mean.

In Sigrid's house, the whole place had been trashed. There had been signs of a struggle and blood leading to the bedroom. Here, everything was perfectly in place, exactly like it had been before the event. It made Cash wonder if Jessica had truly seen something so terrible, or if she'd made a mistake. It was a reach—her shock was very real—but he had to hope. Another murder less than two months after Sigrid was a terrible thing to think about, especially in a place as safe as Salt Cliff was reputed to be.

At the entrance to the dining room, everyone paused, as if they were collectively holding their breaths. The door was slightly ajar. Jessica had probably noticed that, and in her curiosity, likely checked it for a stray guest. It was a room that was off-limits according to the sign that hung on it, and not a place where anyone would really feel the need to go.

From where he stood, the inside was still dark. It would have been easy to mistake a vaguely body-shaped item for a deceased person. Yet, light did spill in from the hallway somewhat. If that really was what was in there, it would've been obvious, even if it was dim.

Cash felt Brian and Amelia standing behind him, a bit too close for comfort. He almost expected them to comically lean over his shoulder to peer past Lucas, who switched on the dining hall's lights. Lucas stood in front of the door for a while, perhaps gathering his courage.

Finally, the four of them stepped forward, forming a line in the room, and there he was, unmistakable, lying on his back on the floor, eyes staring at the ceiling. He was close enough to the entrance that Jessica would have seen him as soon as she'd pushed the door open. He was wearing a navy-blue suit, though his tie was no longer around his neck, and the top buttons of his shirt seemed to be ripped open.

At the same time, there was no blood to be seen anywhere, no murder weapon or really any signs of a struggle; aside from the one chair that was toppled over beside him.

However, one thing was certain. He was most definitely very much deceased.

"It's Orin!" Amelia gasped, clapping her hand over her mouth after a moment of stunned silence.

Everyone was processing that reality. The man who had debated Susan just a few hours earlier now lay dead in the back of the brewery, hidden from those who had attended the event.

Cash's instincts kicked into gear and he turned to Lucas. "You should call the sheriff."

Lucas nodded slowly before he left the room, already dialing a number on his phone. Cash herded Amelia and Brian out to the main brewery area, where Emma had already taken Jessica. Jessica was seated and crying, with Emma across from her, still trying to console her. Brian sank into a chair nearby, looking fairly green with nausea. He immediately hugged himself with both arms, seemingly seeking some kind of comfort.

Amelia seemed a bit more put-together than the others, but her hands were shaking and her jaw tight. She stared out in front of her distantly, like her mind had shut down to protect itself.

Cash didn't blame any of them. This was far more than simply an unusual situation. He was more surprised that he felt calm and focused rather than shocked—though, of course, this wasn't his first rodeo. That in itself was somewhat disturbing. He preferred to never have seen a body at all, and now he'd seen two in the span of eight weeks. It was something he would have never seen coming, and he was surprised that he was managing to handle it so well.

"Okay, we need to breathe," Cash said firmly. He received a nod from Amelia, Brian, and Emma; Jessica kept her head in her hands. "Let's think for a moment and cool down, alright?"

Emma straightened herself. "I'll get some juice. Sugar should help, right?"

Cash wasn't sure, but it looked like Emma needed to do *something* to feel useful, and he nodded at her and let her leave for the kitchen. Jessica still wasn't looking up, but Amelia and Brian both watched Cash expectantly.

"Did either of you see anything strange tonight?" he asked, thinking of the questions that Riley could possibly ask them when he arrived.

They glanced at one another and shook their heads. Amelia was the one who spoke first.

"Nothing," she confirmed. "I mean, there were people I didn't know, sure, but... That's to be expected, right?"

"Yeah, with the whole event, it could be anyone," Brian added, his voice thin. "Like, he left the stage, and he was mingling, and then everyone left. Nothing unusual about that, except that now he's dead."

Cash mulled that over in his mind, along with thinking about everything he'd seen that evening. Of course, he hadn't known that they needed to watch out for a murderer, and he hadn't been paying attention to anything that might have been slightly out of the ordinary.

He thought about whether he'd actually seen Orin after the debate itself and if anything had happened after he'd left the stage. Cash remembered spotting him in the crowd a few times, but couldn't recall him leaving or even heading for the bathroom. Cash tried to go through the event step by step, but there were blanks regarding Orin's whereabouts that he simply could not fill.

"Jessica?" he asked gently, walking over to her as Emma returned and handed everyone a glass of juice.

With a tear-stained face, Jessica looked up at him, accepting the juice from Emma, and took a sip. She was shaking so much that some of it spilled on her shirt, but she didn't seem to notice that at all. She was pale, and her makeup had run down her cheeks.

"Do you think you'd be able to talk about it?" Cash pushed, and Jessica nodded, though hesitantly. "What happened?"

Jessica swallowed back what seemed to be a lump in her throat. "I don't know... I... I saw the door was open, and I called out to see who was in there. Nobody answered, and... I went in, and he was there, so I ran."

"You didn't see anyone else?" Cash pressed, and Jessica shook her head.

"No. But... I mean, I just wanted to get out of there as quickly as I could. I didn't think... I mean, I'm sorry. It was dark."

Cash knew that pushing her further wasn't going to help. He believed that she hadn't seen anything aside from Orin's body itself. She was probably in too much shock to actually pay attention to anything else, anyway. His instincts were telling him to go back to the room himself and investigate further, but Cash knew that he wouldn't be able to get himself to do that. Once was enough.

"Thank you," Cash said with a sympathetic smile before he turned to Brian and Amelia. They seemed to be in somewhat better shape, though the shock was still visible on both their faces.

They glanced at one another, and Amelia spoke.

"I don't know who could have done this," she said. "And I have no idea why. I mean, as far as I know, Orin is a good guy."

"Susan?" Brian muttered, but from the way he said her name, it was clear that he didn't believe she could have done it. "I mean, he's standing against her, right?"

"She also left right after the debate," Amelia pointed out. "Before everyone else. And I still saw Orin around after she was gone."

Cash heard the gate opening, and he turned to see Riley, Lucas, and Pete coming inside. Lucas was pale, but focused; the shock about the situation was obvious on his face, and yet it seemed like he was trying to storm forward regardless. Cash frowned. Riley he had expected, but why was Pete here? Maybe he was after a fresh story, but how had he heard about it? Did he follow Riley to the brewery after Lucas called? Had he seen Riley pass by with his lights on, or did he know more about what was going on?

"Where is he?" Riley asked of the room at large, and Cash was the one who moved to lead him through the brewery.

In the meantime, Lucas blocked Pete off. Cash could hear Pete starting to ask questions, and Lucas trying to field them. But Cash himself was focused on the main situation at hand.

He took Riley all the way to the dining room and let him inside. Unlike the others, Riley did not gasp or look shocked at the sight. Instead, he moved instantly into investigation mode, crouching over Orin and putting on gloves as he started inspecting the body.

"Who found him?" Riley asked, without looking up at Cash.

"Jessica," Cash replied. "But she's in no state to truly answer questions right now, I think."

Riley nodded slowly. "Has anyone else been in here? Touched anything?"

"Brian, Amelia, Lucas, and I came in here, but none of us touched him. Or the furniture."

"Good. Did you see anything strange during the event?"

"No. Nobody else did, either."

"Have you been questioning them?" This time, Riley did look up, and he had one eyebrow raised.

Cash paused, knowing that Riley probably wouldn't be happy with him, but that he also couldn't lie to the sheriff.

"Not extensively," he finally said, and Riley sighed.

"Didn't I tell you not to get in trouble?" Riley got up again, facing Cash with his arms crossed and a strict expression. "You should stay out of this, aside from being a witness."

"Sorry," Cash answered, though he didn't truly mean it. "What do we do now?"

"*You* should go home," Riley replied firmly. "*I* will be getting a forensic team in here."

"You're not going to interview me?"

Before Riley could answer, there was a commotion elsewhere in the brewery. Cash could hear Selena's voice, as well as a few others.

"Where is he?" Selena was shouting. "Show me!"

Riley rushed back to the main part of the brewery, and Cash followed, wondering why Selena was reacting this way.

"Wait, wait, calm down." Riley had reached the brewery's main area, and he was holding Selena back by her arms. "Listen, I know this is terrible news, but I need you to stop and breathe. I can't let you go back there."

Cash stood slightly behind Riley, watching Selena's face. He saw fury there, something far deeper than shock.

"No," Selena insisted. "You can't do this. I'm his *family.*"

Cash was surprised by that. He hadn't had any clue about their connection. If he had, he'd probably have asked her about the accusations before.

"I know," Riley said gently, without releasing his grip. "But I have to do my job. There's nothing you can do to help. You need to calm down."

Selena seemed as if she were giving up, and Riley finally let her go. At this point, she spun on her heels and stormed toward Emma, who was still standing close to Jessica. Selena's shoulders were tight as she shoved a finger in Emma's face.

"This was you," Selena hissed, spittle flying from her mouth and sheer hatred in her tone. "I *know* it was."

"What?" Emma's eyes widened in surprise, and she took a step back with her hands held up in a gesture of peace. "No, no, I'd never—"

"He was exposing your lies, and you wanted him out of the way!" Selena snapped, and at this point, Riley stepped forward again, grabbing her by the wrist and pulling her back. "Admit it! You killed him because he was an inconvenience!"

Everyone was staring now, and no one aside from Selena and Riley was moving. Cash himself had no idea what to do, either. He felt as if it was his duty to step between them, to get involved, but it was possible it would only escalate the situation. He knew that he was supposed to leave all of this to Riley, and he remained rooted to the spot despite his inner turmoil.

"This isn't helpful," Riley said, dragging Selena away from where Emma stood, now backed up into a corner. "Selena, you need to give me a chance to investigate the situation. I'm sorry, but I think it would be better if you went home."

"Home?" Selena turned to him, her eyes burning both with tears and anger. "You expect me to just... Do nothing? Riley, my cousin was *murdered,* and the person who did it is right there! You need to arrest her immediately!"

"I didn't do this!" Emma shouted from the corner. "You have to believe me!"

The argument was quickly escalating, and there were no signs that it was going to slow down. Brian had gotten up from his seat at this point, as had Amelia, but neither of them took a step closer.

Lucas was now moving between Emma and Selena, protecting his wife with his arms out on either side of his body.

"Liar!" Selena screamed as Riley continued to drag her away into the corner. "You pretend to be all sweet and lovely, but the world will know the truth about you!"

This wasn't good. Cash glanced around the room, trying to find a way to distract everyone or to snap the tension, but he couldn't see anything that could do so. At the same time, he didn't want to escalate things.

Riley whispered something urgent to Selena, his expression serious and authoritative. Selena stopped screaming, but her body stayed taut.

For the moment, he decided to trust Riley's expertise.

Chapter 9

"That's enough," Riley finally said, his voice filled with such authority that everyone was immediately silent. "Emma, I'm going to ask you to wait for me in the office. Lucas, you may join her."

The two of them obeyed, while Selena peered at them through narrowed eyes. However, she didn't say anything. It wasn't that she'd calmed down; Cash could see that in the pure fury of her expression. Maybe Riley had threatened to arrest her for obstruction to get her to comply, but he never seemed like that kind of guy to Cash.

"Brian, Amelia." Riley turned to them this time. "Would you mind waiting at the far end of the room with Jessica?"

They nodded and escorted Jessica to the opposite corner. The two of them had to walk on either side of her, each holding an arm. Her legs wobbled as she walked, as if they were going to give in at any moment.

"Cash, please take a seat." Riley nodded toward him with soft eyes before turning away. "Selena, please come with me. Pete, please don't interfere with my investigation."

Cash quietly did as he was asked, watching Riley lead a still-fuming Selena through a side door. Pete stood to one side, making notes and taking a few pictures. Nobody stopped him, probably since they all had a lot on their minds. Cash wondered what the front page would look like in the morning. Would it have another sensational headline, or something more demure?

From previous newsletters, Cash knew that Pete had a tendency toward more flashy journalism, but that felt inappropriate for this situation. He hoped that Pete would, well, read the room.

On the inside, Cash wished that he could be a fly on the wall during the interviews, but he chastised himself for his curiosity. This was a serious situation, and he was, after all, simply a civilian. The right thing to do would be to let the law take its course and not get involved.

He wasn't connected to Orin, either. At least, directly. Riley perhaps could have forgiven him for the investigation around Sigrid, given how close he had been to it. But with this, it was different.

Is it really, though? Cash found himself wondering. After all, Orin had accused Emma of some serious things, and now it was clear that he was also related to one of Cash's employees. There was definitely an argument to be made that Cash was deeply connected to this case. Riley started de-escalating the argument, insisting that they move away from the alley since they were going to disturb the crime scene.

Still, it wasn't his place. He'd already agreed he wasn't going to be involved. Or, at least, acknowledged that Riley didn't want him to be. He wasn't sure how far he could push his luck, and he didn't want to destroy whatever kind of relationship the two of them had—or could have, one day.

Cash was surprised to find himself thinking about that. Had he really started developing feelings for the sheriff, or was it just a little crush? He wasn't sure, but this was not the time to be worried about those kinds of things. For now, he had to focus.

Cash sighed and let his eyes wander around the room. The atmosphere was tense and quiet. The others sat against the wall together, but they were all staring off into space, making no attempt to talk to one another—

Jessica stared up at the ceiling, while Brian and Amelia were looking at the floor.

That was probably an issue. They'd essentially scrubbed part of a crime scene for a killer. A lot of evidence could have been lost in here. What other evidence had they simply missed during the event or after?

Maybe there had been something lying around that should have been suspicious. Something that could give them *some* kind of clue about what was going on. But they'd only cleared tables and cutlery, the standard things to be done in any eating establishment after an event. The main floor was mopped, which meant that footprints could have been lost.

But they hadn't touched that dining room. There had to be fingerprints somewhere, or a handprint, or anything else that could lead Riley in the right direction. Hopefully, their efforts hadn't ruined the entire thing.

With it being quieter and his heart beating a bit slower, Cash started going over the night moment by moment in his mind. The shock was somewhat wearing off, and he felt even more focused.

As far as he knew, Emma and Lucas were both running around all night, serving customers and keeping everything flowing. She wouldn't have had enough time to go off and actually murder someone, unless she had done it during the one or two bathroom breaks she took. Cash doubted that. He didn't think she would have it in her, anyway.

Any kind of evidence that led to her would have some kind of innocent explanation, too. Her fingerprints and DNA would be all over the brewery, as would Lucas's. That wouldn't be enough proof.

As Amelia had said, Susan had left early, and Orin had still been mingling with the crowd afterward. So it could not have been her, even if it did look like she had a motive. All of the staff had been busy in the kitchen and with the food, and after that with cleaning.

Could it have been one of the other attendees, then?

There were people there that Cash knew, and many that he didn't. All of them could have been connected to Orin in some way. Nobody seemed to be acting strangely, at least as far as Cash could tell. Even in hindsight, he couldn't think of a moment where someone's behavior should have triggered red flags.

Nobody had moved toward the dining room as far as Cash knew, either.

When had Orin gone there? Or had he been taken there, given the lack of blood at the scene? Had he actually been killed in the dining room, or somewhere else? What kinds of clues were hiding out of sight?

And if there wasn't any blood at all... Then how had he died? Could it have been natural causes, somehow?

Maybe it had been a professional hit. Someone who had been hired to do the dirty work. In that case, Susan's name couldn't be thrown out entirely, but neither could Emma's. It wasn't a place Cash wanted to start his investigation, given that it would complicate everything.

"Cash, hi." Pete had sauntered over to him while Cash had been distracted.

Cash looked up, and Pete was as effortlessly handsome as he had been that day at the marina. He had a charming smile on his face and sat down across from Cash as if they were having a relaxing hangout at the beach.

"Terrible circumstances to be meeting in again," Pete continued. "But it is nice to see you."

Cash felt a shiver run down his spine. A pleasant one, he had to admit. Still, he had to be careful. Whatever he said now could end up in the newsletter, and he had no idea whether Pete would misconstrue any of it. Pete's eyes looked sincere as he studied Cash, with no indication of an ulterior motive. If he was somehow trying to manipulate people for his stories, then he was far too good at it and that could make him dangerous.

"I don't think I have much for you," Cash finally answered, and Pete immediately chuckled, waving him off.

"Not a lot of trust for the media, huh?" he smiled. "I don't blame you, given your personal history. Don't worry, I'm not here to cross-examine you."

Cash couldn't think of another reason for Pete to be talking to him, though. This wasn't exactly the time or place for flirtation or a friendly chat. But Pete had such open body language that it was disarming. If he was being truly sincere, then it could be helpful to have him as a friend. After all, as a journalist, he had skills and ways of finding information that Cash did not. The fact that he was handsome was simply a bonus.

"Is that so?" he said as he crossed his arms. "Then what can I help you with?"

Pete sat up a bit straighter, but his expression remained friendly and full of natural charm. "I *was* going to ask your opinion on everything, but I can sense that you're not exactly going to leak all of the information you have. So, instead, perhaps I can ask if you'd like to have a drink sometime?"

That offer definitely caught Cash off-guard. It hadn't come out of nowhere. Cash himself couldn't deny the chemistry between them, but he couldn't help thinking that Pete definitely had some kind of ulterior motive.

"Maybe," Cash said anyway. "But you should try asking tomorrow. Right now, I'm a little busy."

Pete got up at that and winked at Cash. "Great. I'll stop by."

He walked off, leaving Cash with more questions in a mind that was already filled with them. He wasn't sure whether Pete actually was interested in him, or whether this was simply a journalism tactic (albeit not an ethical one) to get Cash to break down his walls.

Either way, there were more important things to focus on right now. Particularly, the dead man elsewhere in the building, and whether he was murdered or had died all on his own. Orin was fairly young and in shape, and it didn't seem likely that he would simply have collapsed of natural causes.

At the same time, however, there were no real signs of a struggle, aside from his loosened tie. No blood, either. Cash knew that it didn't look like some kind of violent attack.

Pete had walked over to the others, and he was now talking to them. It seemed like they were more willing to answer some of his questions. Cash couldn't hear what they were saying, but Pete was writing things down in his notes.

Cash wanted to confront him, but Riley came back into the room at that moment.

"Pete," he said, his voice low with a warning. "You should go. This is inappropriate. You can ask everything you need to at the station."

For a moment, it looked like Pete was going to argue, but then he shrugged, nodded, and headed for the exit. Maybe he'd already gotten enough, and he'd simply decided it wasn't worth the effort to fight about it.

Everyone watched him go in tense silence before Riley approached the group at the far end of the room. He checked in with them and asked if they'd be able to come to the station in the morning. They agreed and promised to get home safely. Then, the three of them left together.

Riley disappeared again, leaving Cash alone to contemplate things. Now, he did get up from his seat and headed to the bar to grab a glass of water for himself. He noticed that his hands were shaking a little bit as adrenaline was wearing off and the true shock of seeing another dead body was settling in.

Despite not being the first time, Cash was certain it wasn't something that he could ever actually get used to. Nor was it something he *wanted* to get used to.

The first glass of water that Cash got was gone after two huge gulps, and he poured himself another, sipping at this one more carefully.

It felt like at least another half hour went by before Riley came back, this time escorting Selena, whose face had been stained by tears. She seemed somewhat calmer than she had earlier, though her body was still tense.

"Will you be able to get home safely?" Riley was saying, his voice filled with clear concern. "Or do you need an escort?"

"I'll be fine," Selena snapped, pulling ahead of him. "I'm not that fragile."

She was clearly still furious, probably because Riley hadn't immediately arrested Emma on her insistence. From that reaction, it seemed like she, at the very least, had already been convinced that this was certainly a murder.

"I understand," Riley said calmly. "But you know that you can call me any time, right?"

Selena didn't answer. Instead, she stormed out of the brewery, and Riley let out a long sigh when he finally turned toward Cash. He let his shoulders drop somewhat, and his authoritative mood started to disappear. By the time he sat down across from Cash, it was more like he was a friend connecting after a difficult day than the town sheriff.

"Well, this is not how I thought my evening would go," he joked with a dry laugh.

"Me, neither," Cash admitted with a somber nod. "Frankly, I'd been hoping that witnessing a murder would never be on my list again."

"We haven't determined that this was murder," Riley pointed out. "I haven't seen any signs."

He didn't specify or elaborate on what those signs would be, but Cash knew that he wouldn't. Riley would be careful about what he said, given that he didn't want Cash to start his own investigation.

"In any case," Riley went on, leaning forward. "I have a few questions that I need to ask you. I know it's late, but it won't take too long."

Cash crossed his arms and slowly nodded his head. "Not a problem."

He wanted to add that he'd spend the rest of the night talking to Riley if he could, but he managed to hold back. A flash of Pete's face earlier crossed Cash's mind; the moment when he'd asked Cash to go out for a drink.

"Alright," Riley cleared his throat and sat up straighter, his expression changing to a more serious one. "First, did you see anything out of place at all tonight?"

"I didn't," Cash replied with a sigh. "Event went off without a hitch, and we cleaned up like normal."

"No strangers or people that stood out?"

"Several strangers, but nobody stood out."

"How about Orin himself? Did you notice him leaving?"

"I didn't. I did notice he was gone, but I didn't think much of it."

Cash answered each of Riley's questions honestly, wondering what everyone else had said to the same line of interrogation. At the same time, he was tired and desperately wanted to go home. He kept to the facts and answered quickly.

Finally, Riley had reached his last question and nodded at Cash's answer. Then, his face changed again, his eyes catching Cash's gaze with something deeper. Cash felt the now-familiar flutters in his stomach and shifted in his seat.

"Now, on to another subject," Riley said strictly, without a single hint of a smile on his face. "I believe I told you to stay out of trouble."

Cash almost chuckled, but swallowed instead. "I promise I'll do my best not to get involved."

"You better not," Riley insisted. "If this wasn't natural causes, then it could be dangerous, and... I don't want you in the middle of it."

Cash felt his cheeks heat up at the protectiveness in Riley's tone, but he kept his expression as stoic as possible.

"I understand."

Chapter 10

After checking in with Emma and Lucas, and saying goodbye to Riley, Cash left the brewery. Outside, the night was dark, the moon narrow and even the stars seemed somewhat quiet. Cash listened to his own footsteps in the parking lot, taking in the silence around him.

It was so much different from the lively event earlier in the evening, like the island itself was shocked by what had happened.

Cash got into his clunker of an SUV and drove away, watching the lights of the brewery grow smaller in the distance. Riley, Emma, and Lucas were all still there, and likely would be until the scene had been entirely processed. Cash wondered what Riley would find that he had missed. Was there a murder weapon, or a visible cause of death that they hadn't seen? Had someone left behind a fingerprint, or a shoe print in the mud, or a piece of an old receipt? There were many possibilities, none of which Cash would know about.

And that was going to make his personal investigation quite a bit more difficult. With Riley's warning, he couldn't be caught back at the crime scene, even after it had been processed. He'd need to find a different way to get to the truth.

With this in mind, Cash was fairly certain he wasn't going to be able to sleep very well that night. The whole night was still playing over and over in his head, on top of Riley's strict yet playful warning.

Cash finally stopped in front of Sigrid's home, which was now his, but it was strange to think of it as anything other than his aunt's house.

He had done some things to make it his own, particularly in the study and master bedroom, but a lot of it was still just as Sigrid had left it. He found it too difficult to imagine changing everything, as if that would mean he'd forgotten her.

With his body sore from the hard work and the stress, Cash got out of the SUV and walked up to the front door. There were a few weeds starting to grow in the footpath that he'd have to remove, or hire a gardener to take care of. Sigrid wasn't the biggest gardener in the world, but she did have many plants and trees around the house that she kept in pristine condition. Cash would need a bit of help to do the same.

He rolled his shoulders and stretched his neck to try and get rid of some of the tension before unlocking the house and going inside. He remembered that first time that he'd walked in, the chaos that he'd seen then.

Now, everything was perfectly neat and quiet, simply waiting for him to come back. Cash took a deep breath as he closed the door behind him and moved toward the kitchen. In all the chaos, he'd forgotten to eat anything, and his stomach was reminding him of that fact.

The fridge wasn't particularly full. A few cold meats, a loaf of bread, vegetables, and a tub of Greek yoghurt. Most of Cash's meals now came from leftovers from the patisserie or from Jamie's food truck. But tonight, he'd have to sort himself out.

While he made himself a sandwich, he pondered Riley's warning.

I should listen to him, Cash told himself. *I could get in serious trouble if I don't.*

At the same time, there were so many people close to Cash who were already involved in the situation, and the whole thing was so murky. Maybe this death had something to do with the scandal surrounding Emma, or the mayoral election, or even the ownership of the fishing shack. There were several possibilities, all almost equally likely.

If only he'd had a chance to look at the scene more carefully. Granted, he wouldn't have been able to touch any of the evidence, but he'd have more clues than he did now.

So, I'm assuming that it wasn't natural, Cash thought as he finished making his sandwich and bit into it. *Not that I really have any evidence for that. Why would I think that?*

Why wasn't there any blood, or a struggle, or any kind of weapon at all? Where had Orin's tie gone? Who had been sneaky enough to do this under the noses of the entire town? Were they following him? Did they choose this event specifically, or was it simply a crime of opportunity? Maybe it was just natural causes, and Sigrid's murder caused tunnel vision.

At this point, Cash knew that he'd probably have to be involved in investigating the situation, despite Riley's warnings. Cash *had* to know the truth behind it all. He'd simply have to keep himself under control. He wouldn't go too far, just far enough to get the answers he wanted. After all, talking to people wasn't against the rules, nor was going through a few old public documents in the library.

Having decided that, Cash got ready for bed. At the same time, he knew he wasn't going to get very much sleep—and he was right.

Most of the night, he rolled around or stared at the ceiling, waiting for the sun to rise so that he could get started. But, at some point, he did manage to drift off, though it wasn't long before his alarm woke him up.

Cash, despite sore muscles and a tired mind, jumped out of bed and got ready faster than usual. He'd have to open the patisserie before he did anything else, and see if his employees were alright to work that day. If they weren't, he'd give them the day off and do his own errands while they were closed.

Before he got into the SUV, Cash received a text from Selena, saying that she needed some time with her family before she returned. He texted back, insisting that she take all the time she wanted. Brian and Amelia hadn't sent anything. For now, Cash was going to assume that this meant they were willing to work.

With a sigh, Cash started the engine and reversed out of the driveway. Nobody was on the road yet, but there was an unmistakable energy running through the air. It was somber and somewhat dark, but Cash wondered if that wasn't just his own emotions running rampant.

Both Brian and Amelia were already outside when he arrived at the patisserie, looking somewhat worse for wear.

"Morning," Cash greeted as he approached them. "Are you both alright?"

They glanced at one another, then nodded at Cash. Brian spoke first. "I think we need to keep ourselves busy. Work will do us good."

"Yeah," Amelia agreed with a timid smile. "I think so, too."

"Have you been to see Riley?" Brian yawned. "He grilled me a fair bit. Not a fun time at six a.m."

"Five a.m. for me," Amelia answered. "It's like he never stops working."

"I still need to get to that, but we should get started first," Cash said, opening the doors and letting them inside. He wasn't sure whether he'd go to see Riley immediately. It felt like he had more to do than be interrogated again. He'd already told Riley everything he'd known.

They moved slowly, but with focus and purpose. Amelia headed toward the booths to start fluffing the pillows, while Brian headed for the register to do the morning checks. They were fortunate they had enough items ready for assembly that they could make due with a short, but acceptable supply of pastries and sandwiches. Cash followed Amelia, thinking of gentle but pertinent questions.

"Were either of you close with Orin?" Cash asked Amelia while he helped her get the dining area ready.

Amelia shook her head. "Not really. I mean, I know that he and Selena talked all the time, but I've only met him a few times. Mostly to buy fish from him. I'm a pretty big fan of seafood."

"I see," Cash said as he adjusted a pillow on one of the longer seats. "So you wouldn't know if he had any problems with anyone? Any arguments?"

"Just the one with Emma," Amelia replied after a moment of hesitation. "And Susan, but that's a competition, not an argument. I suppose it still counts, right? I don't know. Maybe someone was angry that he was running against her. Or someone was angry that he insulted Emma..."

Amelia seemed to be babbling to keep her real emotions at bay. Cash could hear the anxiety in her voice and see the discomfort in the way that she was moving. He wondered if he shouldn't be insisting that she went home.

"Anyway, thanks for letting us come in," she continued as if she knew what he was going to say. "I couldn't sleep. Felt like my apartment was going to swallow me whole."

"Well, if it helps you to be here, then I'm glad," Cash said, moving on to another table to get the chairs in place. "If there's anything else I can do for you, please tell me."

"I will."

The atmosphere became quiet after that, with Amelia keeping herself as busy as possible. Brian, behind the cash register, was doing the same. It looked like they had it all under control. Maybe they were trying to keep things as normal as possible so that they wouldn't have to think about what they had seen.

Cash himself, however, was thinking about the answers that he was looking for. He wasn't going to find them here. The first place he knew that he had to go was down to the library. Whether this was related to Emma or not, Kieran would be able to help him find *something.*

"Will you two be alright on your own for a while?" Cash asked Brian when they were finally ready to open.

"Yeah," Brian answered firmly. "I'll let you know if there's anything."

"Thanks."

Cash left the patisserie and drove down to the library, tapping his fingers impatiently on the steering wheel most of the way. Part of him was nervous, looking out for the sheriff's truck as if he was doing something terribly illegal.

But technically, he wasn't getting involved. He wasn't at the crime scene, breaking into people's houses, or interrogating random people. All he was doing was looking to access publicly available records and talking to friends and connections. He'd keep his investigation to that, too. He wouldn't get in Riley's way.

Cash parked right across from the library, which had just opened, and headed inside to find Kieran already behind the counter.

Kieran's eyes widened when he saw Cash, and he hurried toward him. "I heard what happened. How crazy is this whole thing?"

"Very," Cash admitted. "And mysterious."

"Heard a few whispers. People are saying that it definitely wasn't natural causes."

"We don't know that yet," Cash insisted as the two of them headed to take a seat in one of the reading corners. "But... I mean... Things are making Emma look bad."

"So, what are you thinking?" Kieran sat back, his arms crossed and his eyes curious. He put down the book he had been working with on the counter in front of him. It was clear that he was ready for this, maybe even excited to get started on his research.

"Riley asked me not to get involved," Cash admitted. "But... I mean, if this has something to do with Emma, then I have to, right? I promised her I'd find the truth, and I haven't."

The guilt of that was slowly coming back now. He felt like he had already disappointed her.

"That's true," Kieran agreed. "Look, maybe we don't do illegal things, hmm? We keep it to what we can find as civilians."

"That's what I've been thinking. Have you found any records or documents yet?"

"Actually, I reached out to Town Hall." Kieran was beaming now, as if he was excited to go on another adventure. "Looks like there are some things available, but it'll take a while to get it. I'll keep looking here, too, but I'm not sure there will be much."

"Maybe you can find some history here," Cash pointed out. "About the brewery, from when Arthur owned it. Or about their family."

"Mm, perhaps." Kieran tapped at his chin with one finger. "But there's someone else who might know something about that."

A light went off in Cash's mind, and the two of them said the name at the same time.

"Morgan."

"You should go see them," Kieran said. "I'll dig deeper where I can while you do."

"Great." Cash found himself smiling. He'd learned that Kieran was one of the people that he could trust with anything. He knew that Kieran would do everything in his power to find whatever they needed. "I'll see you later."

Cash hurried out of the library, in a hurry to get to Morgan's. He wondered why he hadn't thought to ask them about the brewery earlier. They knew everything about the island's history, and probably knew more about its families than anyone else aside from the records themselves.

The Cedar & Sage Collective gallery sat waiting as Cash arrived. Morgan was standing on the patio, tending to their plants.

"Morgan," Cash called out, and they looked up at him and smiled immediately. "Lovely to see you."

"And you," Morgan replied. "Please, come in. Have some tea."

Cash wanted to dive right into his questions, but he decided on the polite approach instead. He followed

Morgan inside, noticing that they'd put some of Sigrid's donated trinkets on display.

Cash sat down on one of the many chairs and waited for Morgan to return. When they did, they brought two cups of tea and offered him one. He took it gratefully.

"How have you been doing?" Morgan asked genuinely, the worry clear in their eyes.

"I miss Sigrid," Cash admitted, tracing the edge of his cup with one finger. "I wish she was still here."

"Ah, don't we all." Morgan nodded sagely, then studied Cash for a moment. "But that's not why you're here, is it?"

Cash chuckled. "You've caught me. I actually wanted to talk about the brewery."

"A terrible thing that happened," Morgan said with soft, concerned eyes. "Orin was a good boy."

"You didn't see anything odd that night, did you?" Cash continued, leaning forward slightly. Morgan was observant and wise; if anyone had noticed something peculiar, it would be them.

"Can't say that I did." Morgan shook their head. "I left fairly early."

Cash remembered a flash of Morgan saying goodbye that night, though he had been so busy he had barely noticed. If they left long before anyone else, then they wouldn't have a lot of information on that. But it didn't mean they didn't know *something* useful.

"Did you know Arthur?"

"I did."

"How did he get it?" Cash leaned forward with curiosity. "When was it started? Do you know how Emma bought it?"

"Oh, slow down," Morgan said, placing their tea down on a nearby end table. "I'll answer your questions, but one at a time."

"Sorry."

"Well. The brewery was founded in the early twentieth century," Morgan explained. "Arthur actually inherited it. It had been in his family since the beginning. I believe he faced some troubles before Emma placed her offer."

Cash processed that information slowly, mulling it over in his mind. "So, would you say that his family would have been angry that someone else had overtaken it?"

Morgan peered into the distance, thinking, before they answered that one. "I believe they were. It had been given from father to son for many years. It has always been a cornerstone of the island. I am aware that Orin was particularly upset about the situation at first."

Cash frowned. If that was the case, then it seemed only natural that Selena would have blamed Emma. She seemed to be a particularly large source of frustration for Orin. He must have had a grudge from the very beginning. In his eyes, she had stolen a particularly valuable family heirloom.

"Would you like to know anything else?" Morgan pressed. "Or are we going to enjoy our tea and a tale of Sigrid?"

"No, you've been a great help," Cash answered with a short laugh. "Please, regale me. I'd love to listen."

Chapter 11

After his visit to Morgan, Cash decided to check on Amelia and Brian and whether they were doing alright, particularly without Selena's sections of certain recipes. He was sure that Brian knew a few parts by heart, and some they might be able to figure out or maybe do without, but probably not all day. On top of that, it was possible that they might have changed their minds about working and were hoping to close early.

When Cash got back to the patisserie, it was fairly quiet, with only a few cars in the parking area. Most of the town had probably heard about Orin's death at this point; maybe they had all gone to the brewery to satisfy their curiosity. Or they could have headed to Pete's new small office to offer their opinions or ask for information from the only printed media in town.

Inside, there were only a few people having coffee, and one man in the corner booth working on his laptop. The people having coffee seemed to be talking about a planned trip to the mainland; nothing about Orin's death.

Both Amelia and Brian stood at the cash register, watching over everything. Beside the register, on the counter, Cash noticed a brand-new stack of newsletters. Cash was sure that Orin's death would be on the front page, though he wasn't sure about the angle that Pete would have taken.

"Sorry for being gone so long," Cash said, glancing around him. "Looks like you have things under control, though."

Amelia picked up one of the newsletters and handed it to Cash immediately, without any answer and with wide eyes.

"It's rough," Brian said, nodding in the newsletter's direction.

Cash frowned. "I'll read it in the office. Thanks."

He didn't look until he was seated behind his desk, and when he did, he had to take a large breath. The front page only featured an article about Orin's death, and Cash wasn't particularly impressed with the angle that it was taking. It wasn't something he would have expected, even if it seemed to follow on the previous scandal.

NEW ACCUSATIONS WITH MAYORAL CANDIDATE'S SUDDEN DEATH

The headline itself was troublesome enough, but the content was worse. The first few paragraphs simply reported on what happened at the brewery: the event, Jessica finding the body, the sheriff being called, and the place being declared a possible crime scene.

But after that, it went into detail. A few quotes from Jessica, Brian, and Amelia about how shocked they were to witness a scene like that. Then, an official explanation from Riley on where the investigation stood. It noted that a cause of death had not been identified, and that Riley was not yet declaring it a homicide.

The last several paragraphs covered Selena's accusations that Emma was behind Orin's death.

"Everyone was finding out the truth about how she got our family's brewery," Selena was quoted as saying. "And she wanted to silence Orin because of that. It's obvious. It should be open and shut. I don't know why the sheriff hasn't arrested her yet."

It didn't seem like Pete was taking a side in the way that he wrote about it, but surely he knew that this would spread through the town like wildfire. Cash could tell that the story itself was sensational, but aside from the headline, Pete didn't seem to be leaning into it *that* heavily. He noted that all of these were allegations and that nothing was confirmed yet. That no suspects have been officially named, and that Selena was close to the case and could be incorrect.

Maybe Cash's bias was making the whole thing look worse than it actually was. But he felt frustration starting to build. He didn't want to be angry at Selena. It wasn't her fault that she was reacting like this.

Orin *was* her family, and she was grieving. She must have been completely out of her mind when she was told. She couldn't have expected such a sudden death. And now, there weren't any answers about why this happened in the first place. Of course, she'd grab onto the first thing that seemed like an answer.

Cash just wished that thing wasn't Emma. This could ruin her reputation, and, frankly, her whole life. She still hadn't had her version of events published in Pete's articles. Nobody would want to support a brewery owned by a murderer, even if she wasn't convicted. Especially if she wasn't, but the murderer was never found. But he was confident that she didn't have anything to do with Orin's death. Even so, a small voice in the back of his head was trying to tell him that he might simply be in denial.

Could Emma be capable of something like this? Cash truly didn't think so. The brewery was her passion and her dream, but she simply wasn't the kind of person who would take anything that far. Neither was Lucas. He was protective of his wife, certainly, but not to the degree that he would take someone's life.

And in any case, the article itself had also made clear that the death hadn't been ruled either as homicide *or* natural causes yet. It was still very much possible that this had been some freak accident, and nobody's fault at all. Orin must have been stressed because of the mayoral campaign; a heart attack couldn't be completely ruled out. That was what Cash was hoping for, though a nagging feeling told him that there was something more behind all of it.

Cash got up from his chair and began to pace around in his office, hoping that would help his thought process flow better. He had a pen in one hand, clicking it as he paced, creating a rhythm that became white noise in his ears.

So, what do I actually know? he asked himself, flashing through his memories in his head. *Orin thought Emma didn't own the brewery legally. Orin was running for mayor, Susan was running against him. The brewery belonged to his family for many years. Articles and documents on it are tough to find in the library. It's not clear whether this was natural causes or homicide.*

It seemed like it was more and more possible that something was being covered up, and that Orin's death was necessary to hide whatever it was. Knowing that, it was obvious that Emma and Susan would both be reasonable prime suspects, even if it was only circumstantial. Lucas would also be in the crosshairs, given his proximity to Emma.

If it *was* a murder, then whoever had done it was probably going for the "natural causes" look. So this had to be an intelligent person, with access perhaps to medical equipment or dangerous items that wouldn't be obvious. Though that answer would likely only come once the coroner returned with the cause of death; and Cash wasn't sure whether he'd have access to that information without some questionable ethics.

We need the documents, Cash thought. *I know that we'll find something there.*

As he was thinking this, his phone began to ring and it made Cash jump. He laughed at himself to break his own tension and picked the phone up from the desk. Emma's name flashed at the top of the screen, and so Cash answered immediately. He was sure that she was devastated by the article, likely just as much as she had been the night of the death itself.

"Did you see it?" Emma's voice was small and almost broken, so defeated that it made Cash's heart fall. "The article?"

He could imagine her sitting in the lounge of her house, her knees pulled up to her chest and a blanket draped around her shoulders. It was a terrible image to think of, but it would be far worse to imagine her locked up for a crime that she did not commit.

Cash sighed and pinched the bridge of his nose with his thumb and forefinger. "I did. Don't worry, Emma, I know you're innocent."

There was a deep, relieved breath on the other end of the line, followed by a fairly long pause. Cash waited, knowing that Emma was probably in a terrible state. Selena's accusations would hold a lot of weight for the rest of the town, and if the truth wasn't found soon, then Emma would lose everything she'd worked for. Far more than it had been when Orin's were the only allegations targeting her. Her dreams would be completely shattered.

"Please, you have to help me," Emma muttered, a sob filtering through her tone. "You have to show them that

I didn't do this. I don't know how, but... There has to be something."

Riley's face fluttered into Cash's mind for a moment, along with his strict warning not to get involved. Of course, Cash had already been pushing his luck, but he was realizing that it was possible that he'd cross that boundary at some point. Knowing what Emma was up against, Cash knew that he'd do everything it took to help his friend.

"I will help you," Cash answered. "But you have to be completely honest with me, even if the truth is uncomfortable."

Cash could sense Emma's momentary hesitation on the other end of the line. It made him wonder if there was, in fact, something that she might be hiding from him. Certainly, it couldn't be something quite as terrible as murder, but maybe it was bad nonetheless. Still, Cash had to know what the truth was, or this puzzle simply would not be solved. Perhaps it would cause some discomfort or strain their relationship, but he doubted that. Everyone had skeletons in their closet, and nobody was immune to making mistakes.

"Okay," Emma finally agreed in a near-whisper. "I'll answer whatever questions you have. Uhm, I'll put you on speaker, too. Lucas is with me. Maybe he can help."

"Hi," Lucas's voice came through more loudly and confidently than Emma's.

Cash could hear the fury and frustration that lay just underneath the surface. It must have been difficult, feeling as if he couldn't protect his wife. Perhaps he wished that the allegations would have targeted him rather than her, since it seemed like most of the gossip had completely skipped over him. She carried that weight on her own, and he must have felt entirely helpless to stop it.

"First things first," Cash started, running through the questions he'd asked everyone else in his mind. "Do you know if Orin had any enemies? Or... If you have any enemies who would want to frame you for something like this?"

"No," Emma insisted firmly. "I mean, our families have always been close, even after I bought the brewery, except for Orin. He's never really forgiven me for that. And I really don't know who would hate me this much, to do this to an innocent person. I mean... I would hope that nobody from the island would... I don't think..."

She trailed off, and Lucas continued. "Honestly, I've been racking my brains about this, too. But nobody hated Orin, and nobody hates Emma. It makes no sense. I'm thinking, surely it must have been an accident."

"Well, what *exactly* had the argument about the brewery been about?" Cash pushed, sitting on the edge of his desk and fidgeting with the pens in the seagull mug. "All of the information I've seen about it has been fairly vague."

"Orin tried everything, to be honest," Lucas answered this time. "First, he insisted his father's signatures had been forged. Then, he claimed we'd filed the incorrect documents and that the timelines didn't add up. Finally, he was certain that his father hadn't been in his right mind when he made the sale, and that the brewery still belonged to Orin in his father's will. He said that proved that his father never meant to give it away."

"Have you ever seen the will?" Cash questioned. "Had Orin been bluffing about that?"

"I don't think I have," Lucas replied, "and nor has Emma. It never quite got to the stage of litigation. I have a feeling that Orin's lawyer informed him that he didn't have a strong enough case."

"And Orin was the only one involved?"

"I'm not sure, but he was the only one publicly ranting about it."

Cash thought about that. Perhaps there was someone else, a figure in the shadows, someone who had a different agenda against Orin, who knew they could use this situation as a cover. Perhaps it had something to do with the fishing shack rather than the brewery, or some personal affair that had gone wrong.

"No wife or kids or lovers?" Cash asked, deciding to try and go down that route for a moment. It was possible that the death—or murder, if that was what it was—had nothing to do with the election. It was the perfect opportunity for someone with an entirely different motive to jump in. It would be easy to hide true intentions behind the election strife.

"He had a girlfriend once," Emma sniffled. "But as far as I know, that didn't really go anywhere. She moved a couple of years ago."

"Everyone knows he's not really the romantic sort," Lucas added, shattering that theory somewhat. "But it's not impossible that he'd been hiding something like that. He was a particularly private person, aside from the mayoral campaign and the whole brewery thing."

Given that those had been the most public events, they were the only angles of research that were worth going after, at least for the moment. On top of that, Cash wouldn't have to try and break in anywhere if he focused on things he could get answers for more readily.

"Okay, well, listen," he said with a sigh. "I've asked Kieran to look into a few things, and I'll see what he finds. We'll go from there."

"Okay," Emma and Lucas both echoed before they ended the call. The mystery was only getting deeper, and Cash still wasn't even sure where to start looking. One thing was certain however.

Orin *did* have an enemy, somewhere. Someone who was hiding on the island and expertly weaving a web to trap innocents into. Whoever they were, they knew exactly what they were doing. It might be more difficult to find them than Cash had initially thought. Either way, he was on their tail, and one way or another, he would catch them in their lies.

Chapter 12

Cash shot Kieran a text with the updates that he'd gotten from Emma and Lucas. He added that Kieran should try to look for anything associated with Arthur, Orin's father. Maybe if they couldn't locate documents about Orin directly, something from his father would give a bit more insight.

Then he got back to work on the patisserie's administrative backlog, though his mind kept wandering back to the case. From what he knew, Arthur had been in a tough financial situation when he'd chosen to sell the brewery to Emma. The details of that situation and the numbers weren't clear, but it must have been particularly tough given how important the brewery had been to his family.

Had he had no other choices, no other pieces of real estate to sell, or had there been no one interested in the others? The fishing shack? Their family home? Why had Arthur specifically chosen the brewery to sell, and nothing else? There were several questions when it came to that, but those were, perhaps, not quite as relevant as the brewery argument, and who else had been involved with that.

Perhaps there were other areas in Orin's secretive private life, too, that could provide answers, though those might be far more difficult to find. They could be impossible to find through legal means; Cash would likely have to do a bit of breaking and entering, as he'd done before, to really be able to dig deeply into any of that. For now, he was going to do his best to avoid that, since he was sure Riley would not be so forgiving if he caught him.

Cash shook his head and got up from his chair to do a few stretches, hoping it would help him get back to focusing on his job. While he was doing so, he realized just how stiff and tense his muscles were. It wasn't entirely surprising, but he hadn't expected it to be quite so bad. After finishing his stretching, he paced around the office a few times, then sat down again, staring at his laptop screen as if it would magically start doing the work on its own.

For a while, he workshopped some ideas to expand the next month's lunch menu and bread rotation, until, at some point, he decided to grab a coffee from the kitchen. Amelia came in from the front of the patisserie halfway through, and she tapped Cash on his shoulder.

She was frowning when she leaned in to talk to him. Cash raised one eyebrow as he waited for her to speak.

"Uh, Lucas is here to see you," she announced like she was telling a secret. "Should I send him to your office?"

"Please," Cash answered, relieved for the distraction. "Tell him I'll be right with him."

When Cash returned to his office, Lucas was standing against one wall, wringing his hands tensely. He looked up as Cash entered, and the frown on his face was telling. He seemed almost lost in his frustration, like he wanted to explode. He clearly had no idea what to do, and this whole thing was weighing heavily on him. Cash didn't envy his position.

"Emma is in an awful state," Lucas said without greeting. "I feel like I'm losing my mind, and I can't really imagine what she's going through. She's locked herself in the house. Can't step outside without some random person wanting to interrogate her."

"I'm sorry," Cash sighed, crossing his arms. There wasn't much he could say. He understood some of what Lucas felt in that moment, but Emma and Lucas had grown up with these people; almost everyone knew them. When he'd been accused of Sigrid's murder, he'd been an outsider. For Emma, the suspicions and anger must have been so much worse. She probably felt like she had been completely betrayed.

"I really want to help, too," Lucas added. "I'm not exactly a sleuth, but I'll do anything at this point. I can't stand to see her like this. She hasn't smiled even once since... Well, you know."

"Yeah, she doesn't deserve that," Cash said as he picked up a pen to fidget with, clicking it and spinning it between his fingers. "I already have Kieran scouring the library, but he's been doing that since the first allegations came out. Morgan was helpful, but not much in the way of evidence."

Lucas stood quietly for several moments before he tapped at his temple. "What about Susan?"

"Susan?" Cash repeated curiously. The only way that she was involved was as Orin's opponent and as Emma's supposed benefactor and supporter, but it was entirely possible that a fan had gone rogue and "taken care" of him *for* her. It was a different angle, but a helpful one.

Then, Lucas continued. "She knew Arthur pretty well, as far as I'm aware. I think they were friends back in the day. Maybe she could tell you something that we couldn't."

That wasn't something Cash had even considered. Morgan knew some of the story, but not the entirety of it. As someone so entwined with Town Hall, Susan must have heard much more about the legal side of the situation. Plus, if she were actually friends with Arthur, then she'd know more about his own perspective on it all.

Maybe she'd also know who else could be interested in framing Emma; or if any of her own supporters could be involved in the situation.

"Then I should go see her," Cash said, finally feeling as if there was some momentum building in his investigation. "I'll go during my lunch break."

"Thank you," Lucas sighed with relief. "I've been trying to keep myself as low profile as possible, too. I'm getting nearly as much harassment as Emma, to be honest."

Cash nodded slowly. The two of them were somewhat trapped in that way, and it would be particularly difficult for them to investigate on their own. Cash could, in a sense, stay far more under the radar. Nobody would be paying attention to him and what he was doing—aside from Riley.

"Maybe I can go see what Kieran has found," Lucas added, running a hand through his hair. "I feel like I'm going to go crazy staying at home, but hopefully nobody will be grilling me at the library."

"Sounds good," Cash said, patting his friend on his shoulder. "We'll get to the bottom of all of this, don't you worry."

"I know." Lucas began moving toward the door. "I trust you."

He left the patisserie, and Cash watched the clock like a hawk, hoping for lunchtime to come sooner. However, it felt as if time was dragging along slower than ever, and his productivity wasn't really impressive.

Finally, the clock hit 1 p.m., and Cash almost leapt right out of his seat to get moving. He closed his laptop and rushed through to the front of the store, where a small rush was forming. Brian looked at Cash from behind the register and smiled.

"Don't worry, we'll be alright," he said, giving Cash a thumbs up. "I'll call you if we need anything."

"Thanks," Cash answered, offering a small wave in return before he hurried out of the front door. Ever dutiful, the SUV was waiting in its spot in the parking lot. Cash jumped in and turned the key.

The SUV grumbled and gave up.

"Really? Now?" Cash muttered, rubbing at his temples and taking a breath to calm down.

He tried again, but all he got in return was a half-hearted sputter and a tired whine from somewhere in the engine. The SUV was not going to move. At least, not in that moment.

"Honestly, this thing," Cash grumbled to himself as he got out of the vehicle and pulled his phone from his pocket. The first text was to a local mechanic, requesting that he come out later that day for a fix.

Then, Cash called a cab. He stood at the far end of the parking lot, tapping his foot with almost comical impatience. He knew that getting places a few minutes faster wasn't going to make much of a difference, but he couldn't help the deep sense of urgency that had taken root.

Riley probably was putting a lot into his investigation, but official processes were often slow and clunky. It could take months before the true killer was revealed, if not longer, given the state of the crime scene. By that time, Emma's life would have fallen apart entirely, and some people in town would probably believe that she was the real culprit for decades.

Cash couldn't let this go on that long.

After a while, a small, yellow Volkswagen Beetle chugged along happily toward where Cash was standing. Cash recognized it instantly and rushed forward to climb inside. The driver raised an eyebrow, probably curious about the hurry Cash was in, but didn't ask any questions.

Cash kept his eyes on the swinging tree air freshener and the pacifier that were tied around the rearview mirror. At some point, the driver had told Cash the story of the pacifier belonging to her child, and that it was something that reminded her why she had to work hard. The tree, however, had no story attached to it as far as he knew; she probably simply liked the smell of it.

The little car made him feel every single bump on the road, with the only truly smooth street being the one right in front of Town Hall. When the cab stopped,

Cash paid and hopped out like he was late for his own wedding.

By the time he stood in front of Susan's secretary, a short woman with a very tight ponytail and thick glasses, Cash was out of breath.

"I need to see Susan," Cash announced, and the secretary peered up at him with what seemed like a look of suspicion.

"Do you have an appointment?" she drawled, almost annoyed.

"It's urgent," Cash insisted.

The secretary sighed.

"May I ask who is looking for her?"

"Cash Kristiansen."

"Alright."

There was a flurry of typing and a few curt nods before she glanced up at Cash again. "She has a ten-minute window for you. Please go through."

"Thank you." Cash nodded in the secretary's direction before passing her and opening the door to Susan's office.

Her office was just as he would have expected it to be. Large floor-to-ceiling windows, neat, square, minimalist furniture, and an ocean blue and gray color scheme. Susan, in her own light blue pantsuit, with her silver hair and tortoiseshell glasses, fit in with the whole atmosphere seamlessly.

"Hi," Cash said, approaching her table as she got up to shake his hand.

"Cash." Susan smiled, leading him over to a pair of chairs that looked out through the windows. "It's a pleasant surprise seeing you. Please, take a seat."

She took the seat diagonally across from him, neatly crossing one leg over the other and watching him with curious eyes. She was still wearing the polite smile of a government official, but he could see something behind it. A motherly affection, maybe? That was strange to Cash, given previous interactions that he'd had with her.

"How has business been?" Susan asked, keeping her tone light.

"Really good, actually," Cash replied, feeling the slight awkwardness in the air. He knew the two of them didn't have much in common, aside from both being connected to Sigrid. But he also didn't want to leap into the real reason for his visit too quickly.

"I'm sorry I haven't had much of a chance to visit," Susan continued, a light somberness in her eyes. "I should make some time. I'll find a spot somewhere in my schedule."

"Oh, you don't have to do that." Cash waved her off. "Perhaps I'll start deliveries. Everyone on the mainland does that, anyway."

Susan smiled at that. "I remember Sigrid telling me she was planning that when we were together."

Her eyes changed suddenly, as if she'd let something slip that she shouldn't have. Cash found himself slightly raising one eyebrow before he caught himself and cleared his throat. As far as he knew, Sigrid didn't really date. To hear that she'd had a relationship with Susan was even more surprising.

"You and Sigrid?" he asked, keeping his tone light and curious.

"Ah, yes." Susan nodded, the nostalgia filtering through her voice. "It wasn't common knowledge, but... Well, we had always gotten along, and eventually, we both had to admit that the chemistry was there. Unfortunately, I was well aware that I had to keep things under wraps. It doesn't always go over well in small communities, if you know what I mean."

"I do," Cash replied sympathetically.

"Sigrid still wanted to tell the world," Susan said with a small laugh. "She said the people here, on Salt Cliff, would understand. That they'd be happy for us. But... Well. I just never thought they'd want me to be their leader if they knew. Perhaps I was wrong. I miss her very much, you know? I wish I could have stopped it all from happening."

"So do I," Cash admitted as the conversation dwindled to a sad silence.

Susan eventually sat up a bit straighter. "I'm sure you're not here to delve into the past. How can I help you?"

"Actually, I wanted to ask you about Arthur," Cash said, leaning forward in his chair. "Lucas told me that the two of you were friends."

"We were, right up to the end."

"Then you probably know about the problem with the brewery."

Susan nodded and paused for a moment before replying. "Orin had insisted that it was promised to him as part of his inheritance, and wanted to pursue legal action to prove that Arthur was not of sound mind when he sold it. Orin used the ridiculously low sale price as evidence for that. It went nowhere, though I'm sure that the documentation must be around."

Emma hadn't mentioned the sale price when Cash had spoken to her. If it truly was that low, then Orin's anger could, perhaps, be somewhat more justified. Maybe there had been someone else just as disappointed in the sale, and perhaps they were after whatever else Orin actually *had* inherited. But if that was the case, then why would they have waited this long to get rid of him?

"If you'd like," Susan continued. "I could pull a few strings to see if I can find those for you."

"That would be amazing," Cash breathed, feeling the tension loosen from his shoulders somewhat. "I'm sure they'd have answers for me."

Susan's computer pinged with a message. She got up to check it, then let out a sigh.

"I have another appointment now," she said, sounding disappointed. "I'm sorry. But I promise that I'll look into the documents for you."

"That's alright, I understand." Cash pushed himself up out of his seat and moved to the door, looking over his shoulder for a moment. "When you have a few minutes for me again, I'd love to hear more stories about Sigrid."

He noticed the light in Susan's eyes as he left, and the sly smile that she wore on her face.

Chapter 13

As Cash left Town Hall, he shot a quick text to Lucas.

Check other property records for Arthur, and who is connected to them. Should be in the library archives.

He got a thumbs-up emoji in return. Hopefully, Kieran and Lucas would be able to unearth a list of names for them to look into.

Maybe Susan could have helped with that, too, but Cash didn't want to put too much on her plate. She was probably one of the busiest people in the entire town, especially with the whole mayoral election now being in complete chaos. She probably hadn't slept much the past few days. People weren't really looking at her as a suspect as far as Cash knew, but as one of the top officials in the town, they likely *did* want a lot of answers that she simply didn't have.

Then there was the sale price of the brewery. Susan hadn't mentioned exactly how much it had been, but her use of the word "ridiculous" indicated something very far below market value. If it was that low, then it would make sense why Selena and Orin had been upset about it, and why she would believe uncovering it would negatively impact Emma. It was a decent enough motive.

Why didn't Emma tell me about that? Cash wondered, hoping that there hadn't been other things that she had been keeping from him. If there were, then what could her reasons have been?

Maybe they were personal, but it did seem like an important detail. The whole problem between Emma and Orin was definitely more personal than political in the first place. Cash wondered if he would need to question Emma again, or if she'd shut down entirely if he did. It could be that this was the reason she hadn't given him her own set of documents yet. Would the answer be in the property records or in the documents that Susan had mentioned? It was likely.

Cash decided that he'd wait a while to see what Susan could find, instead of confronting Emma. It was possible that she simply hadn't thought about that in the midst of all of the pressure hanging over her.

"Cash?" The question in his name made Cash turn, pulling him out of his musings entirely.

Pete was standing on the sidewalk, holding a thick stack of papers. His hair looked different in the sunlight; lighter, almost to the point where it seemed like it was glowing. Even his eyes had a brighter glint in them, and his smile made a knot tighten in Cash's stomach. He wore a loose tan shirt and jeans, different from his usual leather combination.

"Oh, Pete, hello," Cash answered, wanting to kick himself for how his voice broke in the middle of the greeting. He cleared his throat. "Sorry, I didn't see you standing there."

"No worries, I get lost in thought too," Pete chuckled, patting the papers in his hand. "I was going to file these to get the newspaper up and running, but..." He stopped talking and let his eyes run over Cash. "Maybe I could take you for that drink first?"

"I can't," Cash said quickly, feeling his ears heat up. "It's the middle of the workday."

The excuse sounded almost lame, but it was the only one he could think of. He wasn't sure *why* he was looking for excuses, anyway. Pete was handsome and charming, and so far hadn't shown any signs of being a terrible person. In all honesty, a quick break was possibly a good idea.

"A coffee, then," Pete smiled. "Or even an orange juice. Whatever you'd like."

"Okay, sure," Cash relented with one hand in his pocket, an attempt at being casual. "But I don't have much time. Lunch is almost over."

"Twenty minutes should do the trick." Pete winked, and Cash found himself laughing despite the tension he was holding in his neck due to the last few days. "Come on, there's a spot right up the road."

Cash walked along with Pete, noticing Pete's relaxed stride and the way his legs seemed longer than they were because of it. His entire aura radiated the confidence of someone who knew themselves and knew the world, too. He carried the papers as if losing them would be a minor inconvenience at most.

The two of them settled in at a small table in front of one of the little tourist shops that dotted the main road of the town. It was dressed up in a French theme, with detailed metal furniture and tablecloths covered in French words and pictures of stamps. Normally, it wasn't a spot that Cash would have paid a lot of attention to, but he knew that those were often the ones with surprising offerings.

Pete placed the papers under the floral table arrangement to protect them against the breeze and leaned back in his chair, still watching Cash with those observant eyes. It made Cash feel as if Pete could see all the way to his soul and find what was lying dormant there.

"Look," Pete started, stretching out one hand to put it on the table. "I hope you're not too mad at me for publishing Selena's side of the story. Just doing my job, you know? I don't think there's anything good that comes from hiding stuff like that. And, well, she might be a bit bitter, but that makes sense. She and Orin were very close."

Cash looked at him with a hint of suspicion. "I'm sure your readers liked it."

Pete laughed and shook his head. "I suppose it did help the numbers. But I mean it, Cash. Good journalism is important to me. I've tried to talk to Emma, and to Riley, but they won't even answer a single text."

"Does that mean you want their opinions from me?" Cash crossed his arms defensively. "Because I won't give them to you."

"No," Pete said, with an unexpected seriousness in his tone. "I don't want to question you, or to get some kind of a story from you. I just... I want to get to know you, Cash. You're... intriguing."

That statement caught Cash completely off guard, and he wasn't quite sure what to make of it. It seemed like casual flirting, but there was something more behind it. It could simply have been Pete turning up his charm, or a hint of what was underneath the masks that he wore. Cash, however, didn't know him well enough to figure out which it was.

Before he could answer, however, a server whose nametag read "Penny" appeared at their table out of seemingly nowhere.

"What can I get you boys today?" she asked brightly, positivity almost bubbling over from her entire demeanor.

"I'd love one of those lemon-lime concoctions you're so famous for, dear Penny," Pete said, eliciting a giggle from her. "Cash?"

"I'll have the same."

"Certainly," Penny smiled before she bounced back into the café.

"You'll love it," Pete insisted, his attention entirely returning to Cash with an intensity that made Cash want to melt under it. "It's got a sweetness to it, but the lemon balances it out nicely. It's incredibly refreshing on a busy day."

Cash watched Pete's face, looking for any sign of deception, but he couldn't find any. If this was an angle that Pete was taking to chase his story, he was definitely doing it expertly. It was possible, of course, that he was being sincere, but Cash couldn't entirely trust that this was the case.

From what he remembered, Pete had almost always been in some sort of trouble, whether with neighbors or the law. Most of the time, he'd talk his way out of it, or simply get a slap on the wrist or a stern word from his father. It was always as if the rules that applied to most people simply could not reach Pete himself.

There was the one arrest that Cash had found a while earlier, which could have been the reason that Pete had finally left the island years ago. It would have made sense that his father made him leave, too, given that image had been everything to the previous mayor. So much so that he was willing to murder for it.

"Oh, I know," Pete said, as if he'd read Cash's mind. "You remember me as a scoundrel, a naughty little boy who always got himself neck-deep in something mischievous. I promise you, though, I'm reformed. Mostly."

He laughed, and the sound could put anyone at ease. Somehow, it was working on Cash. He allowed himself to feel more relaxed, to let his shoulders lie back and his muscles loosen. Maybe he could let go a bit more around Pete, if he made sure to pay attention to any indications of an agenda.

"I'll see about that," Cash said, this time with a sly smile of his own. "Leopards don't really change their spots, do they?"

"This one did," Pete insisted, shifting himself so he was sitting up a bit more straight. "The world out there taught me some valuable lessons. I don't ever want to go back to who I was then. I know it's tough for people around here to give me another chance, and I probably shouldn't be asking for one. But, Cash... I just want to prove myself. Surely you can understand that?"

Cash did understand that. There were still people on the island who didn't fully trust him; not because he had been a murder suspect at one point, but because he was an outsider. Pete left and came back in the middle of a scandal that had his family as its central point. It made sense that people wouldn't immediately take him in again as one of their own.

That was especially true given what had happened just over a month earlier. People would be wary of anyone connected to him.

Maybe that was why Pete had been drawn to Cash in the first place. They were both standing on the outside looking in, feeling both part of and separate from the island community. Plus, it could also be that Pete believed it would be easier to get close to Cash, who hadn't been around for most of the troubles of his earlier life.

"I suppose so," Cash answered, measuring his own words. "Alright, Pete. I'll give you that chance."

Pete grinned as Penny arrived with their drinks: light green liquid in a tall glass with ice, drops of condensation already forming on the outside. As soon as Cash took a sip, he could already tell that Pete was right. It was delicious.

"You like it?" Pete asked as he pulled two ten-dollar bills from his pocket and handed them over to Penny. "Don't worry about the change."

Penny seemed enamored as she looked at Pete, thanked him, and slowly walked away again. It was a big tip, too. Cash took a few more sips before he answered.

"Yeah," he said. "It's really good."

"Great, then I know we can come back for more," Pete replied, taking a big swig from his own glass without using the straw. "You know, when you have a bit of time."

Something clicked in Cash's mind; something Pete had said earlier, and suddenly, he had a burning question. "You said Selena and Orin were close?"

Pete nodded. "Very. She'd been just as upset as he was about the brewery thing, maybe even more. She'd pushed him hard to get the law involved. But as far as I knew, all of that was in the past. Honestly, I thought it was all pretty much resolved before Orin mentioned it in his campaign."

If that had been the case, then Selena must have had a few answers herself. But she hadn't reached out aside from calling out of work, and hadn't said anything aside from her accusations in the newsletter. Then there was Emma, who had been similarly secretive about the sale price.

It made sense that Selena would be so upset, especially if she and Orin had been close. She was grieving, and she probably didn't want company around. But Emma... Maybe she knew more than she was letting on.

"To tell the truth, Selena had been pretty loud about it back then," Pete went on, shifting in his seat again. "But she never mentioned anything when the dust settled."

Cash thought about Selena's reaction the night of the murder, and the way she had immediately assumed that Emma was behind it. Something was hiding beyond that argument, something that no one was truly willing to bring to light. Cash wasn't sure what exactly it could be, but he knew that he had to find out.

"She mentioned it now," Cash pointed out. "It's all over your front page."

Pete shrugged that off. "To be honest, I'm not entirely sure the whole story tracks. I'm sure there's a lot she hasn't said. And there has to be a reason that Emma won't talk to me at all, right? I don't know, it's messy."

"You can say that again," Cash sighed, before checking his phone. "Time's almost up. I should finish this and start heading back to the patisserie."

"Sure," Pete answered, though he did look a little sad about it. "But promise me we'll do this again."

"Mm, no promises."

Cash stayed long enough to finish his drink and laugh at a few more of Pete's jokes before he called a cab again to head back to work. He didn't really have the energy to walk right now. The same little Volkswagen showed up, and Cash sat in the back, getting another curious look from the driver.

The case took a short backseat in Cash's mind as he thought about what exactly was happening between him and Pete. As he thought about it, Riley's face flashed through his head. The whole thing made him sigh deeply, and he noticed the glance the driver gave him in the rearview mirror. But she didn't ask any questions, and Cash was grateful for that.

He didn't exactly have time to be trapped in some kind of love triangle, but he was overthinking it. It could be better to simply go along with whatever happened, and to cross whatever bridges he needed to when he got to them. For now, he had other things to focus on, anyway.

Chapter 14

For the rest of the day, Cash was finally able to let his work distract him. He dove into catching up with the administrative side of things and spent some time in the kitchen assisting the others. It was about four p.m. when Amelia called him to the front, saying that Albert, the mechanic, had arrived.

Cash immediately got up from behind his desk and hurried out to the parking lot, like a worried parent heading to see the pediatrician.

Albert stood in front of the SUV, rubbing his hands with a rag that had seen better days. He wore blue coveralls and thick brown work boots, and the sun glistened on his mostly bald head. He was deep into his fifties, a highly experienced professional whose entire life revolved around cars, from what Cash had heard. Beside him stood a proud toolbox, likely filled with anything that could possibly be deemed useful on a callout.

Cash hurried over to him, the keys to the SUV already in his hands. "Albert, thank you for coming out."

"Mm," Albert grunted, nodding in the direction of the vehicle. "Been a while since I've seen this one. Must've been looking after her well."

"I try," Cash replied, feeling fairly proud of himself. "It won't start today, though. Not sure why."

"Mm," Albert grunted again, holding out one hand, and Cash handed him the keys. "I'll get her going."

"Thank you." Cash watched as Albert unlocked the SUV, got in, and tested it; it still wouldn't start up. Albert nodded and grumbled something to himself before patting the steering wheel. He didn't say anything else to Cash, simply popping the hood and starting to fiddle around with pieces of the engine that Cash couldn't name.

Cash, however, stood where he was, wondering if Albert knew anything about Orin's family. He'd probably worked on their cars before, but had he ever had an actual conversation with any of them? Had he known Arthur?

If he did, when would be the most appropriate point within this appointment to ask about it? Cash wasn't sure whether Albert would answer any questions at all. He didn't seem to be the most talkative person, and as far as Cash knew, wasn't interested in much aside from engines.

For about twenty minutes, Cash watched Albert working, and at the end of that time, he got in and started the SUV without any trouble. A small smile formed on his face as he got out and handed the keys back over to Cash.

"She's alright," he announced as if he'd performed a life-saving procedure. "No charge."

"Really?" Cash asked, surprised. "Not even a call out fee?"

"I'll have something to eat," Albert answered. "Sigrid's food is payment enough."

Cash almost laughed at that, but nodded instead. "Sure. Can I ask you something?"

"Mm," Albert muttered, though it was clear he was in a hurry to get that bite.

"Did you know Orin's family?" It was the best question Cash could think of in the moment.

"I did," Albert said thoughtfully, though he only elaborated briefly. "Too many skeletons."

With that, he walked past Cash and up to the patisserie. Now, Cash had many more questions than he started out with, but it was fairly clear that Albert wouldn't be particularly interested in answering them.

Cash followed Albert inside, but headed back to his office to get back to work. Once the patisserie closed, Cash stayed for another hour before finally deciding that it was time to go home.

Being alone with his thoughts, Cash drifted back to the afternoon with Pete, the few minutes with Susan, and the way that the brewery situation had become ever more mysterious.

Lucas had texted him that they might have found a few records, but it would take time to go over them. He'd added that he'd gone home, that Emma needed him, and that he'd search through things while he was there. For now, Cash would have to wait; something that he didn't particularly enjoy doing.

Cash sat in the living room for a while, planning his next day and thinking of who he needed to question next.

Selena was the first name to pop into his head, but he felt guilty at the idea of reaching out only to basically interrogate her. The last thing she needed right then was to be constantly reminded of the past. Then, there was her family; but the same was true for them, and Cash didn't really know any of them, either. Frankly, he had no idea how many of them were on the island or connected to the situation in the first place.

Pam probably wouldn't know any more than she'd already told, and Morgan wouldn't know very particular details.

It felt as if Cash had hit a wall in his investigation. Without the details of the documents and without more information, there was nowhere to go.

So, I have no choice, he thought, impatiently tapping his foot on the floor. *I'll have to just... wait.*

Beyond the investigation, there was Pete. And Riley. And Cash's confused feelings about both of them. It was something that he didn't want to overthink, but he couldn't help himself. He wondered if either of them were actually acting on feelings, or if he was simply seeing things. Was the chemistry real, or was he just hoping that it was?

There are more important things to be focusing on, Cash chastised himself in his head, and got up from his seat. He sauntered to the kitchen to make himself dinner; something simple. Macaroni and cheese, a dinner he'd had many times when he still lived in the city. It was quick and easy and filled him up.

In the back of his mind, he could see Sigrid shaking her head at him for making a mess during his first attempt at making the simple dish in her kitchen. The thought made him smile. For what seemed like the millionth time since she passed, he wished that he could see her again. Her last call hadn't been a good one, and he'd been too late. If time could have been reversed, he could have stopped it all from happening.

Thinking like that won't help anyone, he reminded himself as he sat down to dig into his macaroni.

The rest of the night passed in more quiet contemplation, and Cash found himself tossing and turning in bed when he finally went to sleep.

By the time he woke up to the lightening sky, he hadn't gotten much sleep at all. Getting ready for his day, he noticed the dark circles already forming under his eyes and the way his shoulders were slumping slightly.

And I thought island life would be relaxing. He chuckled at his own little joke as he combed his hair into place and straightened his posture.

Cash checked his phone several times before he finally left the house. He headed to the patisserie, where Selena was already waiting outside the front door with Brian and Amelia. Cash was surprised, not expecting that she'd want to be back at work so soon.

"Selena," he said as he approached them, and she looked up. The bags under her eyes were far more pronounced than his, and she was obviously pretty out of sorts. "What are you doing here?"

"I needed to get out of the house," she answered, fidgeting with a loose thread on her shirt. "I just... couldn't take it anymore."

Cash reached out to squeeze her arm. "Okay, I understand that. But tell me if you need to go home, alright?"

"I will. There's one other thing... There are a lot of things I have to organize for the funeral, and the insurance, and other stuff. Is it okay if I take and make those calls? I'll do it in the kitchen, not in front of any customers."

"Of course," Cash said quickly before unlocking the front door. "Anything you need."

Selena was quiet after that, moving through the motions on autopilot, while Brian and Amelia regularly shot each other worried glances. Cash still felt half asleep and in desperate need of a good cup of caffeine.

There was still a little time before the patisserie opened, and Cash remembered seeing Jamie's bus close by on a corner, where they had been setting up for the day.

"Think I'll head out for a coffee," Cash told Brian, who was busy working on getting the register ready. "Let me know if there's an emergency."

Brian nodded, and Cash noticed the sidelong glance that he got from Selena. It made sense that she'd be a bit disappointed; she was used to being second-in-command, even if Brian did a lot of the admin, and having him take over that place was likely not something she would be okay with. But right now, Cash didn't think that she needed that extra pressure on her.

Without saying anything to her, he left the patisserie and took a walk down to where he'd seen Jamie's bus. They were still setting up tables on the curb side, but a grin spread over their face as soon as they saw Cash and they bounced over to him.

"Hey! You're here early," they pointed out. "Looks like a storm, too. What's up?"

"Rough night," Cash answered. "In need of your best coffee for a pick-me-up."

"Oh, I'm on it," Jamie said with a quick wink. "Here, perfect spot with a view."

They led him to a table which looked over the hillside, and Cash sat down, realizing that a headache was building up. He rubbed at his temples, thinking that he'd grab something from the first-aid kit back at the patisserie when he returned.

Jamie returned with the coffee and took a seat beside Cash. "It's still quiet. If you need someone to listen, I'm here for you."

"Ah, thanks." Cash smiled. "I'm not sure there's much to talk about, really."

"You seem worried," Jamie pushed a little harder. "Is it Selena? I saw her pass by here earlier. I didn't think she'd be back at work already."

"Mm," Cash agreed, surprised that Jamie was so observant. "She's taking it very hard, and, well, she's said some things about Emma that I simply don't think are true."

At this point, Cash wasn't sure *who* to believe at all. He still believed in Emma's innocence, but he was sure that Selena had good reason to say what she did. Whatever was still hiding under it all had to have the answers.

"Well," Jamie said, stretching the vowel out like they were trying to find time to think. "To be honest, I was wondering if there wasn't any anger still there. I mean, Selena was furious about the sale when it happened. She pushed Orin and got their family to work on it together. She was all over town petitioning to stop the whole thing. Told everyone that Arthur was out of his mind. I'm not entirely sure how many people believed that then, but I think a lot of their family did."

"Any of the family still on the island?" Cash questioned, wondering if this could be a possible new angle.

"Selena and an uncle, I think. George was his name." Jamie pondered the answer for a few moments longer. "I think most of the others have moved, though they'll probably be back for the funeral. I think another cousin had been visiting recently, but I'm not sure. Honestly, I don't know them *that* well, I'm just retelling what I've heard from customers here."

"Of course," Cash said. He felt a little silly for not trying to take advantage of that kind of knowledge earlier. Maybe he'd have known more if he himself had spent more time with customers rather than in the office. Then again, eavesdropping was morally gray at best.

"Anyway, I'm not surprised Selena reacted like this," Jamie shrugged, getting up to fix up the rest of the tables around Cash. "She's always been passionate about family matters."

That made sense. At the same time, Cash knew that he was going to have a difficult time balancing his need to protect Emma with his responsibilities as Selena's employer. He'd thought that he was starting to grow closer to Selena in general, and something like this could badly affect the workplace environment.

Right now, however, he didn't feel like it was the right time to approach the topic. He'd have to simply behave carefully and manage his own reactions.

Cash drank his coffee slowly, wondering how he'd get a hold of this George or the other cousin. The family would be around for Orin's funeral, but that wasn't exactly the place to start interrogating people. Timing would be everything if he did end up trying to question them.

"Have you heard anything else about it all?" Cash asked when Jamie passed by him again, and they cocked their head for a moment.

"Not much," Jamie admitted as they put their hands in the pocket of their apron. "Some people do believe that Emma could have killed Orin, some don't. Some people think it was George, since he used to be jealous of Arthur, but he's been ill himself for a while now, so I don't know. Oh, and I think someone mentioned some kind of argument about Arthur's house in the family. They wanted him to sell that instead of the brewery, and he refused."

"I see," Cash said. He rubbed at his chin, thinking about all of that. He hadn't known about the argument about the house or about George. If he was sick, then of course he wouldn't be able to wrestle a healthy man like

Orin, but there were more ways than that to murder someone.

Cash checked his watch and took out some money from his pocket to pay Jamie. "I should get back to work. Thanks for the coffee."

"Always a pleasure," Jamie answered, already clearing the mostly empty mug from the table. "I'll see you again!"

"Yeah, bye!" Cash greeted and started making his way back up to the patisserie. He wanted to know more about George and the rest of the family. Maybe Albert was right. Maybe they had far more skeletons in their closet than anyone was aware of.

Chapter 15

When Cash reached Fjord & Fika again, Amelia was at the front, dealing with the earliest customers, while Brian was seating another couple. They seemed to be doing better now, less shaky and pale, more focused. It looked like work actually was helping them, which made Cash feel relieved. Cash didn't see Selena until he passed through to the kitchen.

She was standing against one of the counters with her phone to her ear. "No, we don't want that many flowers. Just on the casket... No, I don't care what George told you, he's not in charge of this."

Selena glanced up at Cash and gave him an apologetic look. She seemed even more tired now than he had seen before. Her entire outfit was now out of place, as if she'd been running around all day.

It was pretty clear that she had a lot on her hands. Cash didn't think he'd find a spot in her day to talk about George or the rest of her family, and perhaps that wasn't right to do, anyway. It was possible that he could ask

Susan, but she barely had a few minutes at a time to spare.

"Don't worry," Cash said to her as he passed by. "Just do what you need to."

He headed back to his office to try and run through a list of names of possible people to talk to.

Pam, maybe? Cash wondered, sitting back in his office chair and placing his fingertips together to focus. *If she knows so much about Orin, she could know about his family, too.*

It was possible, though everyone had described Orin as private. Did that mean that he didn't spend much time with his family, either? But if that was the case, then he wouldn't be so close to Selena, unless she was the only person he really spoke to. Maybe he had more feuds with people on the island than Cash had thought.

If he did, then there were more suspects, too, and more reasons for his possible murder. Cash wasn't sure whether that was a good or a bad thing. On the one hand, it gave him more avenues for leads; but on the other, it could make narrowing things down far more difficult.

Cash decided to try calling Emma one more time, to see if she knew anything else about the rest of the family, but he only got voicemail. He couldn't blame her for switching off her phone; she'd probably gotten so much harassment that she felt she had no other choice. Lucas was another option, but he didn't answer either.

Kieran didn't know the family personally, so he'd not be able to answer a lot of questions about them. Morgan would know about building histories and cultural stories, but wasn't the kind of person who paid a lot of mind to gossip. They probably wouldn't be too knowledgeable about the more soap opera-like parts of the family's heritage.

"Hey, Cash?" Selena had appeared at the door. She spoke in a soft, somber tone, and her face looked forlorn. "I've got to go down to the funeral home. Some things can't be done over the phone, apparently. I'm sorry."

"Don't worry about it," Cash answered kindly, smiling up at her. "We've got the place covered for now. You should be focusing on your family."

"I know," Selena sighed, putting her hands on the back of the chair across the desk from Cash. "It's so frustrating. The coroner hasn't said anything yet, and Riley doesn't want to give us any updates, either. I don't know what to do at this point."

Those were more missing pieces of the puzzle: the cause of death, and whatever Riley had uncovered in his own investigation. Cash couldn't touch those avenues. Riley definitely wouldn't offer him any information, and he'd be furious if he found out that Cash tried to talk to the coroner. He couldn't go to the crime scene, or to Orin's house, either.

"I'm sure they're doing their best," Cash replied to Selena, even though he knew it wasn't helpful. "Listen, I'm sorry about everything. You should take whatever time you need. Your job will still be here when you're ready, and I'm here if you need me."

"I appreciate that," Selena said tensely. "I have to go. I'll be back later."

"Of course," Cash agreed, and he watched her leave. He wondered if there was a sneakier way to get the coroner's reports, although every way he could think of was certainly illegal. He needed to be careful. He couldn't let his curiosity win over reason.

It was a while later that Cash got a text from Lucas, asking if he could come by in the afternoon for a talk. He hadn't added anything else, but Cash was hopeful that he and Kieran had finally found something in the library's archives. Cash answered in the affirmative and checked the clock on his phone. It was almost ten-thirty. At least an hour and a half before the afternoon even started, and probably much longer before Lucas would actually arrive.

Cash sighed and ran a hand through his hair, wishing again that he could somehow make time move faster.

Instead of sitting tensely waiting without being able to focus on his job, Cash decided to go to the kitchen to see if he could help out there, again. It was the one place where he found a bit of escape from the storm brewing in his mind.

"She's not doing great," Amelia said when she saw Cash. She was standing by the oven, watching a batch of sandbakkels. "I told her she should probably go home, and she just wouldn't."

"I won't make her," Cash answered with a sigh. "But I think I agree she should be taking more time off. Not because she could make mistakes, just because it looks like she really needs it. Stress like that is really hard on a person."

He remembered the first few days after everything had calmed down when Sigrid passed away. Cash had been in her house alone several times, and the weight of it all had been so heavy that he felt as if he would collapse. It was a feeling that would still come to haunt him often when he was on his own, when his mind wasn't busy enough. Until the end of that situation, adrenaline had kept him going, but after that, all there was was this enormous emptiness in his soul.

Amelia walked toward him and wrapped him in a hug. She didn't say anything, but Cash did feel his emotions well up at the physical nature of her care.

He swallowed that back and stepped away. "Thanks, Amelia. Are you doing alright? It can't have been easy for you, either."

"I'm fine," she said, though her tight smile betrayed her. "We've got to stay strong for each other, right?"

"True," Cash answered as the timer on the oven pinged. "Let me help you get those done."

They worked mostly in silence, which suited Cash well enough. He was trying to think of more questions he could ask Lucas when he got there, mostly about Orin's family. Emma's family were closer to them, but perhaps Lucas had heard a few things through the grapevine. Cash knew Lucas would be eager to answer questions too, and maybe less likely than Emma to keep things hidden.

Then again, maybe there were some things that she hadn't told him either, though Cash was fairly certain that Lucas was just as involved in buying the brewery as Emma had been. If that was the case, then why was she the one more targeted? Was she the only one who pushed the sale? Was her name the only one on the deed? It didn't seem likely. So, what was the real reason?

Cash continued adding the curd to the center of the cups of the sandbakkels. They were testing a new curd in them, trying a few new flavors to see if they sold well. Of course, the classic lemon with the patisserie's signature basil twist was still everyone's favorite, but Cash had a good feeling about the strawberry. He was pretty sure that even Sigrid would be impressed with it.

Elsewhere, Amelia started with another batch of pastries. Soon enough, Brian would take over for his section and the part of Selena's that he now knew. It was a smoothly oiled machine, even with the hiccups of mostly losing one of its parts.

Cash found himself wishing that this was all that life was. Just spending time in the kitchen, baking, taking a breath, and building connections. Unfortunately, it seemed like things would never be that simple for him.

He spent the next couple of hours in the kitchen, even skipping lunch, though Brian insisted that he sit down for a moment to at least enjoy a muffin. Cash did so, which got approval from both employees, before jumping back into the work. A few times, he ventured out to the front to greet customers and to see if he could catch any whispers of gossip.

Unfortunately, none of the conversations he heard had anything to do with the death or the town's suspicions; they were mostly friends catching up or tourists talking about how fantastic the island was.

Around two, Cash spotted Lucas's van in the parking lot, and he felt a little guilty at the combination of relief and excitement in his heart after half a day of tense anticipation. Cash met Lucas at the door and immediately ushered him through to the office, where they sat down across from one another on either side of the desk.

"Coffee?" Cash offered, and Lucas nodded. He had a briefcase with him, one that looked like those that would be carried by businessmen in a 90s film.

Cash hurried off to get both of them a mug, and when he returned, Lucas was sitting with his head in his hands. It seemed like he was doing so more out of exhaustion than hopelessness. His hair hadn't been combed that morning, and his usually neat clothes were somewhat wrinkled. Even his beard was growing haphazardly; it was clear that the whole situation was tough on him.

"Thank you," Lucas said when Cash placed the mug on a coaster in front of him. "Been a long day. Barely had any sleep last night... again."

"I believe that," Cash sighed as he took his seat again. "How's Emma doing?"

"She hasn't left the bedroom yet today," Lucas admitted, letting out a heavy breath. "Barely even eats. I wish I could do something more."

"So do I," Cash replied, glancing at the briefcase. He had a feeling that whatever was in there was going to lead to some kind of breakthrough, even if it didn't hold everything that they needed.

"Okay, so," Lucas straightened up, placing the briefcase on the desk and slowly opening it as he spoke. "Kieran and I think that we might have found something, but I don't know how helpful it will be."

"That's good news," Cash said, though he tried to keep his voice as even as possible. It felt as if the waiting game had been going on for far too long.

Lucas retrieved several sets of documents from the briefcase and spread them out on the desk. "We found Arthur's will. Or rather, his *wills.*"

Cash peered at the documents, picking up two that looked like copies of one another. As he read through them, he noticed that parts were missing; in particular, those sections that indicated who had set up and signed the wills. However, at the top, both documents noted that this was Arthur's last will and testament.

"Copies?" Cash asked, looking at the second page of each document.

"Not exactly," Lucas answered, tapping at one specific line on one, then the other. "Look at this. The numbers don't match up. The dates are the same; just before the sale."

Cash took a closer look. He noticed what Lucas was talking about. One of the wills had the market value of the brewery nearly double what the other indicated.

"And then here's another," Lucas pointed out. "The date is later. It's probably the final one. It doesn't have the brewery on it, but the shack, on one of them, is valued higher, too. But I couldn't make out who the beneficiaries were on any of these. It cuts off halfway through sentences."

"I wonder why that is," Cash pondered, trying to see if there were any other inconsistencies in the documents. However, aside from the obviously changed numbers, everything else was exactly the same.

"Well, I remember that Town Hall was digitizing a lot of things a few years ago," Lucas answered tightly. "But in that process, there was a burst pipe and a lot of documents were damaged. I assume that the information was lost at that point."

"Seriously?" Cash muttered under his breath. "Still, this is valuable. Someone must have changed that information deliberately."

"Kieran and I thought so too." Lucas shifted in his seat. "Someone must have forged one set of documents and tried to replace the real ones. Maybe they were interrupted or the whole thing was lost in the system. I don't know. But whatever is going on here, it's probably related to Orin's death."

"Definitely," Cash agreed, getting up from his chair to pace behind the desk. "Whoever forged these will absolutely be linked to whoever could have killed Orin... You know, if he was killed. We need to find out who it was."

"But how?" Lucas had a demand in his voice, along with fresh tiredness. "Kieran is looking into it, but it's possible that no other documents can be definitively connected to these. Even if we have suspicions on who it could be, that's circumstantial at best. Whoever is behind this, their tracks have been covered for them."

"Wouldn't your lawyer have access to one of the original documents?" Cash pressed, trying to find any route to the truth. "If we have that, then we'll know which of the numbers are more accurate. That's a step in the right direction, isn't it?"

"I'll try to get a hold of him," Lucas agreed, suddenly more confident. "Maybe he'll know who the valuator was, or knows an accountant, or whoever. I'm not sure, but it's definitely better than nothing, isn't it?"

"Yeah." Cash paused his pacing and put his hands on the desk, staring at the documents. "Do you and Emma have anything with these numbers on them?"

"I'm not sure," Lucas admitted. "I do know we bought it for a lower price."

"It should be on the purchase contract. We can compare that with the market value on the will."

Cash was quiet for several moments before he spoke again. "But, well, this is more than we've had in a while. It's a promising lead. We should keep going."

Lucas opened his mouth to answer, but suddenly, his phone began to ring. Lucas pulled it from his pocket and looked at the screen. Then, he frowned.

Chapter 16

Cash watched as Lucas answered the call. "Jamie? What's going on?"

Cash couldn't hear what Jamie was saying on the other end of the line, but he noticed how Lucas's face paled instantly. Every bit of color had drained from him, and he held the phone so tightly that it seemed like he would crush it in his hands. Whatever Jamie had told him, it must have been completely terrible news. Several possibilities ran through Cash's mind, but he tried to quiet them. He wouldn't react until he knew with certainty what was going on.

"You can't be serious," Lucas said, his voice trembling. Cash wasn't sure if it was with shock or with rage; both seemed equally possible. "I'll get down there right away. No, I'm not waiting for them to call me. Thanks for telling me."

Lucas slowly pulled the phone away from his ear and ended the call. With dead eyes, he stared at it for several long moments. Cash stood completely still, waiting for what looked like an explosion about to happen. Lucas remained seated for a few seconds more before he got up very deliberately, every movement stretched for longer than usual.

Cash expected him to take a swing at the wall, or to throw his phone, but Lucas did neither. He paused before looking over his shoulder at Cash. His eyes were dark and hard now, pools of pure fury.

"That was Jamie," Lucas said, and the words that followed turned into a hiss. "The sheriff has arrested Emma."

The shock hit Cash all at once. First, he wasn't sure about what he had heard, but he managed to process the words eventually. His eyes widened, and he felt his jaw tighten. It didn't make sense. Emma hadn't done this, and the only evidence that Cash was aware of was either gossip or circumstantial. He couldn't imagine that it was even possible for Riley to be convinced that she was guilty.

Cash could see the anger bubbling in Lucas's face in the way that his mouth moved and his eyes hardened.

"I can't believe this," he muttered. "I can't believe he would do this to her."

"Wait," Cash said, lifting his hands and stepping forward. "We have to stay calm. There has to be some kind of misunderstanding here."

Lucas let out a dry laugh and threw his head to one side for a moment before facing Cash again. "Misunderstanding? *Misunderstanding?* Riley has arrested my wife! What kind of *misunderstanding* is that?"

With every repetition of the word, Lucas's voice grew louder, harsher. He seemed like he was on the verge of losing his mind. Cash knew that he had to de-escalate the situation, but he wasn't sure that was even possible. He didn't want Lucas to do something stupid, something that could derail everything that they'd been working on.

At the same time, he was angry and hurt about the situation, too. He felt confusion and uncertainty, and his mind was running at a million miles a minute. From Lucas's face, it looked like he was ready to break Emma out of jail, and a part of Cash wanted to do that, too. But acting rashly wasn't going to be helpful. They couldn't find the truth if they were all in prison.

"Okay, okay," Cash tried, starting to gather the documents together. "Listen, we don't know what's going on yet."

"You're right," Lucas said. His tone was a dangerous one; the calm before the storm. "I'm going down there right now. Riley will have to answer to me."

"You shouldn't do anything rash right now, Lucas." Cash's reply was measured and careful. He didn't want to tip emotions over the edge. "You have to focus. You need to be calm. I know it isn't easy, but you can't let your anger take over. Don't make this worse than it already is."

"Are you coming with me or not?" Lucas snapped as he curled his hands into fists at his sides. "You're welcome to stay here if you want, but I'm not just going to let this slide."

Cash quickly realized that he couldn't let Lucas go alone. The situation was tense enough. If he was there, maybe he could have time to talk some sense into his friend. He couldn't stay behind, anyway. He wanted answers, too. But he knew that they wouldn't get anything by force.

"Alright," Cash relented. "I'll drive, okay? All I'm asking is that you stay calm."

"I'm not promising anything," Lucas retorted, but he did lower his shoulders and loosen his fists.

That was better than nothing. Cash put all of the documents into one of the desk drawers, locking it and placing the key in his pocket. They couldn't risk someone finding them, even Cash's employees. All that would do would ramp up the town gossip, and the truth could easily be lost.

Lucas had already left the office at this point, and Cash rushed after him. He noticed Brian and Amelia's surprised faces as he passed, but he didn't have the time to explain what was going on. He'd be back when he knew more.

Lucas stood by the side of the SUV when Cash reached it, clearly bristling. His usually pleasant face had turned completely red, and his entire body was tense, like he was gearing up for a fight. Cash didn't know what to expect once they finally reached the station, but he knew that it wouldn't be good. Lucas was already toeing the line of fury, and it wouldn't take much to push him right over it.

Cash got into the SUV, hoping that it would cooperate, even just this once. Lucas got in next to him, and Cash turned the key.

To his relief, the SUV chugged to life, and they were on the road. The drive was completely silent, though Cash imagined that Lucas had a lot of unsavory comments in his mind. For a moment, Cash considered switching on the radio, or even opening a window, but decided against it.

Lucas stared out of the front window, and even his side profile was intimidating in this state. Cash doubted that it was a good idea to go to the station at all, but he couldn't blame Lucas for wanting to. Even Cash felt a deep unease and a disappointment in Riley for doing this in the first place. But there had to be some reason. Riley wouldn't do something like this without at least one solid thing on his side.

But... What could that even be? What had convinced him to bring Emma in in the first place?

Had Cash been wrong this entire time? Had he, and even Lucas, been completely fooled by an act that Emma had put on? Could she really have been responsible for something so terrible? Cash hated thinking that way, but he had to admit that there was a lot pointing in that direction. He couldn't let himself be blind to any of the evidence, even if it was something he didn't want to be true.

Cash knew that Riley might not want to offer any real information on his reasoning in the middle of an investigation. But he did hope that Riley would, at least, be empathetic toward Lucas's struggle. Maybe they could at least speak to Emma and check in with her, see if she was alright. If they could, then perhaps that could soothe Lucas's anger somewhat.

After what felt like an eternity, Cash pulled the SUV into the parking lot in front of the Sheriff's office. It looked like no one else had heard the news yet, since no crowds had formed outside. Not even Pete had shown up at this point. That was good. They didn't need to have some kind of dramatic conflict in front of the entire town.

Lucas immediately started fiddling with the door to unlock it, almost seeming to vibrate with rage.

"Lucas," Cash started, a warning in his tone. "Don't lose your temper. We'll find out what is going on, I promise, but you have to stay calm."

Lucas shot him a furious look, but didn't say anything. He got out of the SUV, and Cash followed, hurrying to lock the doors before rushing up the steps. Cash reached out to grab Lucas by the arm, but missed, and

Lucas threw open the front doors of the office with impressive force.

"Where is she?" Lucas demanded as he stormed inside, getting the attention of the receptionist immediately.

There was no one else in the front room, and Lucas's voice thundered against the walls. The receptionist's eyes widened. She glanced at Cash with recognition in her eyes, but quickly turned her attention back to Lucas.

"I'm not sure what you mean, sir," she said, her voice even. "Please calm down, and I will do my best to assist you."

"Don't lie to me," Lucas answered, walking up to her counter, but staying about two feet away. It seemed like he was struggling to control himself, yet still doing his best to do so. Cash stood closer, ready to intervene if absolutely necessary. "My wife. Emma. I know she's here."

"Sir." The receptionist tried again. "I can't help you if you won't calm down. Please understand."

"Just get the sheriff," Lucas hissed, though he had managed to lower his voice. "He's arrested my wife for no reason. I want to know what's going on. Get him out here."

"Please wait a moment," the receptionist said, before pressing a button on her desk. "Sheriff Thompson? There's someone here who wants to see you. He's saying his name is Lucas. Seems... Upset."

"I'll be there in a moment," the answer came, sounding as if it was said over an ancient radio. "Please ask him to take a seat."

"Forget it," Lucas grumbled. He stood where he was, crossing his arms.

The receptionist seemed to give up on trying, staying quiet behind her counter and simply focusing her attention on the computer in front of her. Cash remained beside Lucas, feeling the tightness of the tension in the air at the very center of his chest.

A minute passed by in intense silence, and then another, before Riley appeared from his office door. He had his hands up in a peaceful gesture, and clear empathy in his eyes, but his shoulders were squared and his demeanor authoritative.

"Lucas, please come to my office, and we'll talk about this," Riley said carefully.

Lucas had a fire in his eyes. "Riley, you better take me to my wife right now."

"I can't do that," Riley answered with a firm shake of his head.

Cash glanced over his shoulder. There were people outside now, gathering to peer through the glass doors to see the drama unfolding inside. "Lucas, let's go with him."

Lucas turned to face Cash. His jaw tightened, but he nodded. "Fine."

The two of them followed Riley through to his office, the atmosphere heavy around them. In the office, Riley stood behind his desk, while Cash and Lucas both remained standing on the other side. Cash closed the door behind himself, hoping that the sound wouldn't travel too far. He knew that Lucas probably wouldn't be particularly focused on controlling his volume.

"Riley," Lucas said immediately once the door closed. "You better explain what's going on right now."

"Listen, I know this must be hard for you—"

"You don't know anything about what this is like!" Lucas snapped, the muscles in his entire body clearly tightening. "How could you possibly know? What is wrong with you?"

"I have to follow the evidence," Riley insisted, his hand hovering over the taser at his side. "And this is where it has brought me. There was enough to bring her in, Lucas. I know it's shocking, but that is the raw truth."

"What evidence?" Lucas's tone rose, pure anger almost overwhelming him. "This is bull, and you know it! Emma didn't do anything wrong!"

"I can't tell you," Riley admitted tersely. "This is an active investigation."

"She's my *wife!* I have the right to know!"

"I'm sorry."

"You have to let me see her." Lucas grabbed at his head with one hand in frustration. "You can't keep her locked up alone like this."

"That's not how this works." Riley stood closer to the window of the office, staring out through the back of the building.

Cash could see Riley's own frustration in his body language, the way his shoulders very slightly sagged and how his head dropped. It was clear that he hadn't wanted to do this, either, but that duty had won out over personal feelings.

"Then how does it work, huh?" Lucas sounded more defeated now, but his anger hadn't faded in the slightest.

"You just grab whoever you want off the street? Whoever is the suspect of the day?"

"No." Riley turned, leaning back on the windowsill with his hands. "I have to follow protocol. I can't let you back there, Lucas, no matter how much I want to. That's how the rules are."

Lucas slammed his fists on the desk, tears now appearing in his eyes. "Where is your humanity, Riley? Have you given it up for your little badge?"

"Lucas, wait," Cash finally interrupted, standing forward to put his hand on Lucas's. "This won't get us anywhere. You need to breathe."

Lucas looked at him with hurt in his eyes, and Cash waited for the next move, his whole body on pins and needles.

Chapter 17

"What do you want me to do here?" Lucas muttered, his eyes catching Cash's intently. "Do you want me to just give up? Just walk away and let my wife suffer for something that is not her fault?"

Cash stole a glance at Riley, who simply looked away. He likely didn't really know what to do in this situation, either. He knew both Lucas and Emma fairly well, even if he didn't entirely consider them his friends. It couldn't have been easy for him to make this decision.

Cash wondered what Riley was thinking in that moment. He wished that he could talk with him honestly, ask him the truth behind his own movements. But he knew that wouldn't happen, just as much as Lucas was not likely to forgive him for this. Cash felt somewhat torn, sitting in the middle of it all, but he knew he had to do all he could to try and get Emma out of jail.

"No," Cash finally said, taking Lucas by the arm. "I *promise* you that we will figure all of this out, but it won't help to lose your temper now."

Lucas's shoulders slumped, defeated entirely. "But what about Emma? I can't just leave her here."

"There are ways you can help her," Cash insisted, starting to make his way toward the door. "Come with me. We'll find the answers. Staying here will only waste time. She is waiting for you, but you have to do this the right way."

Lucas didn't say anything, but he did reluctantly leave with Cash, following him demurely through the offices and back out the front doors. Outside, there was now a fair crowd of nine people, whispering to one another and staring at Lucas and Cash when they left the building.

"Ignore them," Cash insisted, guiding Lucas in the direction of the SUV. People were turning toward them like a mob wanting blood, but Cash refused to look at them. Lucas seemed to be struggling, but he followed Cash's lead reluctantly.

"What's going on?" someone yelled, the demand echoing across the growing crowd.

"Has she really been arrested?" asked another voice. "Did the sheriff find something?"

"Is it true? Did she do it?"

"I knew it!"

Lucas didn't turn toward them, but Cash could see his hands shaking at his sides. Cash himself wanted to shout at them to shut up, that they didn't know what they were talking about. But he managed, barely, to hold himself back. He focused on the way the sun moved through the clouds and onto the ground to keep himself calm.

The two of them got into the SUV, and Cash waited before starting it for a moment so that they could both catch their breath. Lucas's shoulders began to shake, and Cash could hear the sobs that he was trying to suppress.

They needed to get their focus back. They couldn't let this development shake them. There were still things that could be done. Emma had been arrested, but not convicted. She was safe with Riley, even if it wasn't in comfort. Nobody could get to her where she was now.

They still had time, even if it wasn't a lot. The arrest could convince more people of her guilt, which could permanently damage the brewery's reputation.

"What do we do now?" Lucas eventually muttered, looking down at his hands in his lap. "Everyone is going to think she's done this now. I know that she didn't. You believe us, don't you?"

He turned his head over to Cash, his eyes puffy and his face red. Cash nodded. "I'm here to help you."

"Then what's our next step?" Lucas swallowed and pushed himself upward in his seat, deliberately pulling his shoulders back and straightening his posture. It was a clear attempt at gathering his courage in an incredibly emotional moment.

Seeing Lucas like this was difficult for Cash, who knew Lucas as laid-back and relaxed. He'd been visiting Lucas and Emma often, and he'd never seen anything close to this anger in Lucas.

"Those documents," Cash said, trying to get his own thoughts back into line. "They're important. There has to be more. That's our key. Was Kieran still looking when you left?"

"Yeah." Lucas locked the SUV door and clicked his seatbelt into place, clearly ready to get going. "Let's move."

Cash started up the SUV and pulled out of the parking lot. He noticed that people were still staring, but he ignored that. They couldn't let the town's fickle ire get to them right now. Emma was probably in an absolute state in the holding cell, and they needed to get her out of there as fast as they could. Waiting for Susan or anyone else wasn't really an option anymore.

"If we can find the real number," Cash thought aloud as he drove. "That's one step forward. If we find a name, that's another step. There might be more connections to other documents. As long as we find enough pieces, we'll have the picture in our hands."

"With three of us," Lucas added. "It'll go faster. I just... I can't let her stay there."

"I know."

The conversation died down again, and Cash left Lucas to his thoughts. There were other buildings in Arthur's will, too. If they could find who else they had been left to, then they'd have a name. Orin was likely the only inheritor of the fish shack, but what about the house and life insurance? It was likely that Orin had lived in the home, but was he the actual owner, too?

And if they found those documents, would the numbers and dates line up? If so, then they could narrow down the names even further.

Cash drove more quickly than usual through the winding roads of the town, careful to keep his focus on the road. He wanted all of this to be over with just as fast as Lucas did, but he knew that they couldn't rush it. Mistakes would cost them more time, at the very least.

Finally, they stopped in front of the library, and when they got out of the SUV, the world was almost eerily quiet, as if it had been waiting for them to arrive there. Cash locked the door, and they approached the library entrance. There weren't many people around here, which was a relief. There would be no one harassing them or asking questions. It was a safe enough place to be, given the circumstances.

Cash walked inside first, with Lucas behind him. Kieran was returning books to the shelves, but he turned around at the sound of the doors opening. He was smiling at first, but it quickly faltered as the two of them approached.

"What happened?" Kieran immediately passed them and locked the front door before returning and sitting with them in one of the reading corners. Around him, the lamps softened the intense lighting of the library somewhat. It was comforting and relaxing, and just enough to slow down Cash's racing heart.

Kieran stared at Lucas, then at Cash, his eyes filled with deep concern. He was waiting for them to explain what had happened, leaning forward in his seat with his hands on his knees and one foot impatiently tapping.

Lucas seemed unable to speak, so Cash took the lead. "Riley has arrested Emma."

Kieran gasped and slapped his hand over his mouth for a moment. Cash saw the pure shock in him; he definitely believed that Emma was entirely innocent, too. It was obvious that, just like Lucas and Cash, he hadn't expected that something like this would ever happen.

"Are you serious?" Kieran finally asked when he dropped his hand. "Why?"

"We don't know," Cash replied and ran a hand through his hair before putting both hands on his knees. "Riley won't tell us."

"He's out of his mind," Lucas added then, speaking mostly through his teeth. "I don't know what he thinks he's found, but this is unforgivable. She hasn't done anything."

"I believe you," Kieran insisted, reaching out to pat Lucas's arm. "And we'll prove it."

"Exactly," Cash agreed to encourage Lucas. "The truth is here somewhere."

"I've gotten through a lot of things," Kieran mused. He was already on his feet again, beginning to walk in the direction of the archive. The library itself almost seemed to echo Kieran's voice from the walls, and the lights seemed to flow along with him. It was a cozy place, bright and airy, and if the situation had been different, Cash would have taken a book and a seat to relax.

Lucas and Cash followed as Kieran continued to speak. "But at least this far, the wills were the only things I discovered. Still, there's a lot more here. Maybe we can take a box each, work through one at a time. It'll take a while if there's more deeper in, but... Many hands, lighter work."

They moved down into the archives, which were quite a bit darker than the library above. There were yellow fluorescent lights on the ceiling, leading all the way back among shelves of old documentation, but they were somewhat dim. Beside the door were two desks and two chairs, one of which was already filled with things that Kieran had been rifling through. The other seemed to be waiting for an occupant.

"I'll get another table and chair ready," Kieran said. "You two get to work."

He clapped his hands together and hurried off back down the hallway. Lucas took the seat that Kieran had occupied while Cash found an unsearched box to open on his table. He sat down and started going through it. This one contained files full of old newspaper articles, none of which were organized according to any kind of system that he could recognize.

This could be harder than they thought it would be. Some things were sorted through properly, thanks to Kieran, but a lot was still simply left as it had been placed.

"This is going to take forever," Lucas muttered as he read through what was in front of him.

Cash sighed in agreement. "We just have to get through it."

He checked his phone; no urgent messages from Brian. That was good. Hopefully, Fjord & Fika would be alright without him for a while. At this point, it was likely that they would have heard about Emma and would assume that that was what Cash was dealing with.

He considered asking the two of them to close the patisserie, but he didn't really think that was a good decision to make. For now, as long as they could handle it for a few hours, he'd leave it be. If Brian told him that they weren't coping, things would change. Either way, Cash couldn't leave Lucas and Kieran to deal with all of this alone.

Lucas could easily miss crucial information in his state, and Kieran couldn't go through everything fast enough by himself.

Cash picked up the first file and started leafing through it. The first articles were particularly old; older than Cash himself. Then a few were from several years later. He was tempted to put the whole thing aside, thinking that everything was probably too old in this file. But he had to be as thorough as possible. Something could be hiding in between the rest of the information, or had been hidden in a place they could find easily, but someone else would not.

Can't skip over anything, he told himself, paging to another article. This one was actually about the brewery. It had an old picture of it, looking much different from how it did now, but it was obviously still the same building. It did seem like part of it hadn't been built yet back then, and the front gardens weren't there.

Otherwise, it was strikingly similar. A man, which the image text indicated was Arthur, stood proudly in front of the building with his arms spread wide. The article explained that he had inherited the place from his own retired father, and that he was excited for a new chapter.

It probably wasn't specifically related to what was happening now, but it was better to have it just in case. Cash set it aside gently, careful not to tear the aging paper.

Lucas leaned closely over his pile, and Kieran was now setting up a desk just behind them. He headed off to get a chair, too, and Cash returned his attention to the rest of the articles.

It took some time to get through the entire file, and there was nothing else in there. Cash reached for the second and checked his phone once again. No messages.

The second file had nothing at all in it, except for a short excerpt on the fish shack, which Arthur had apparently bought rather than inherited. That was set aside. Nothing in the next file, nor the next. Cash worked through the last one, already exasperated, and once again, found nothing.

Slowly, time crept by in the dim room, and it was tough to tell where they were in the day. Cash knew, however, that they were staying into the night, since, at some point, Brian did message him to let him know that they had actually closed the patisserie already.

At some point, Kieran got up and returned with a mug of steaming coffee for each of them. By now, Cash's eyes felt like they weren't seeing things quite right. He rubbed at them a few times and stretched his arms and shoulders.

The document-analysis life wasn't really for him, Cash had to admit that. But it was probably the most important part of this entire investigation. They had to find *something,* something more than small articles and half-written documents. It was there, whatever it was. Maybe what they found on its own wouldn't be enough to prove Emma's innocence, but it could cast doubt or find another suspect for them.

"Wait," Kieran paused the entire operation with that single word. Both Cash and Lucas turned in their seats. "Look at this."

They moved their chairs to sit closer to him, all peering down at the document he had in his hand. "It's a valuation statement for the brewery, and a copy of an even older will. It was hidden in between a bunch of book donation statements."

"Let me see," Cash said, and Kieran offered him the documents. "The dates are different. Look. The valuation is newer. Wait... Newer even than the other wills? They're six weeks apart."

"It says the higher valuation on there, too," Kieran pointed out. "But all of the names have been blacked out."

"And it was with completely different documents," Lucas added, and all of them clicked what that meant at the same time.

"Someone was trying to hide these," Cash finally said, leaping up from his chair and gathering the simple articles that they'd all found as well. "Whoever they are, they have to be involved. We need to figure out what these hidden names are."

Chapter 18

"Someone forged the second will," Lucas muttered as Cash cleared one of the tables to put all of the articles side-by-side with the will and the valuation statement. "And they forged the valuation. Otherwise, how could the will have an earlier date than this? They wanted it to be valued higher."

"Orin would have benefited from that," Kieran said, rubbing at his chin. "But who else? The person whose name has been taken off? It does look like they might have gotten a share of the brewery, too."

"Then why kill him now, and not back then?" Cash wondered. " And if they benefited from it together, why would they want to eliminate him? Were they afraid of all of this being uncovered?"

"That's the only thing that makes sense," Kieran replied. Lucas nodded in agreement. "It could have been, if he had kept up his accusations against Emma.

He might have known about these documents, and where they were."

"We'll need to get a list of the family members who were on the will in the first place." Cash could feel a sense of excitement building up. This was the breakthrough they needed, and enough evidence for Riley to at least consider that someone else might be at fault for Orin's death.

The three of them jumped when Cash's phone suddenly rang. They each let out an uncomfortable, dry laugh when he answered. "Susan?"

"Cash! I need to talk to you," Susan said urgently on the other end of the line. "It's important."

Cash heard a tone indicating that another call was coming. "Susan, I'll call you back. Soon. I promise. Stay by the phone."

He ended the call and checked the name of the new caller. It was Amelia. That was odd. She should have left the patisserie hours earlier, and he couldn't imagine what other reason she would have to call him. She could have heard something from a customer, or might have wanted to check in about Emma, but both of those were things she'd have preferred to text rather than call about.

"Hey, Amelia, what's up?" Cash asked with concern.

"Uh, I just drove down the road that goes up the hill by the patisserie," she babbled, sounding nervous. "I saw the lights were on up there, but I swear Brian and I shut them off earlier. I don't know if someone is breaking in, but maybe you should check it out? I don't know... I really think we shut them off."

Cash frowned, and his jaw tightened. "Alright, thank you for telling me. I'll be right there."

"Sure, bye." Amelia ended the call, leaving Cash somewhat confused. He knew that they were on to something here, but he wouldn't forgive himself if something were to happen to the patisserie. He had to go see what was going on.

Meet me at F&F in 20. We can talk there. He shot a text to Susan before turning back to Kieran and Lucas. They were watching him with a mix of curiosity and tension. Both looked ready to leap into action, but Cash didn't want them to join him.

"I have to go," Cash announced, glancing down at the documents that they'd found. "Can you two get all of these together and meet me at the patisserie? We can check them out in detail there, along with the others."

"Alright," Kieran said. He raised an eyebrow. "Are you going to be alright on your own?"

"I'm sure everything is fine." Cash wasn't sure that was true, but with Lucas's temper as high as it was, Cash thought that it would be better if he went alone. It seemed unlikely that things would escalate; perhaps Amelia and Brian had simply forgotten about the lights. But she had been so sure they hadn't, and maybe someone had caught wind of the investigation. It could be a simple distraction to buy time, or something worse.

If it was someone with bad intentions who had learned how close they were getting to the truth... Well, then the answers might be coming to Cash and his friends quicker than they'd planned for. If not, then Cash could simply check in and ensure that everything was closed properly.

"Seriously," Cash continued when he noticed the incredulous look in Kieran's eyes. "Look, I promise I won't do anything stupid. If there's any sign of danger at all, I'll call Riley."

"Okay." Kieran still didn't sound convinced, but he relented. "We'll be there soon."

Cash still hoped that the situation with the lights was a simple mistake, but during his time on the island, he'd learned that almost everything went deeper than he thought. It was possible that this was no different. It was better to be prepared for any eventuality, anyway.

"See you then," Cash said to Kieran and Lucas, even adding a casual wave to convince them that this wasn't that big a deal.

He moved out of the space between the desks and stepped out of the archives. As he climbed the stairs, the brighter lights of the library above hit his eyes, and for a moment, it was almost overwhelming.

Cash squinted as he fully came up into the main library and waited for his eyes to adjust before he kept walking to the front door. He could feel his heart beating in his ears, and his hands were already somewhat clammy. It seemed like recently, anxiety was as normal to him as breathing; maybe something he would have to mention in his next therapy session.

Outside, the streetlights were on and the night was dark, though lit up by the vast expanse of stars above. There were no clouds now, and the breeze was light. In other circumstances, Cash would have paused to take in the beauty and calm of it all. As it was, however, he only felt a tight fist gripping his chest.

He wanted to head to the patisserie, quickly switch off the lights, and get back to the investigation. That was the best-case scenario, but he could feel that something big would come from the documents they had found.

Perhaps even bigger, given whatever it was that Susan wanted to tell him. Perhaps the information that she had would make everything click into place.

Cash walked up to the SUV and unlocked it, getting in and hoping that it would still be willing to work with him. The first turn of the key didn't result in anything, and Cash swore under his breath.

Okay, pause, he told himself. He sat back in the driver's seat and closed his eyes, taking several deep breaths and counting to ten. He knew that he had to keep his head on straight, no matter what happened, and no matter where his thoughts tried to spiral to. If he wanted to do this right, he had to focus, and he had to stay calm.

"Right," Cash muttered when he finally opened his eyes, and he tried to start the SUV again. This time, it took a second, but the SUV started up, and Cash could get moving. He was grateful for that. If he'd had to wait for a cab, whoever could be at the patisserie would have time for whatever plot they had, or they could simply escape without a trace.

He drove slowly, gathering his thoughts and organizing the clues that he'd found in the documents in his mind. He thought of the dates of each will and how they corresponded—or didn't—with the valuation that they'd found. Were those dates in themselves significant, or were they simply a coincidence? Had the forged versions of the documents actually been filed on those dates? Were they hidden without any officials ever seeing them?

The list of questions that Cash had was only growing at this point, but at least, so was the list of answers. He was getting closer, something he could feel at the pit of his stomach.

Luckily, the road was quiet and there was no traffic. Cash hadn't even checked the time, but he guessed that it was around 9 p.m. The vintage Suzuki's clock was broken and had never been much help, but the placement of the moon, full and bright in the sky, gave him a fairly good indication.

Another thing that was adding to Cash's anxiety was the possibility of running into Riley. He wanted to ask him why he'd arrested Emma and where the investigation itself was. The coroner must have determined that the death was a homicide if there was an arrest in the first place; that much Cash had assumed. But anything else, in terms of the evidence Riley actually had and the rest of his thoughts on the case... All of that was a mystery.

Cash looked up when he reached the road leading up the hill, the one that Amelia had mentioned. From here, he couldn't see the patisserie very clearly, but he could see that the lights really were on.

Okay, that might not be good, he thought as he continued up the winding road. To one side, the island stretched out as the SUV climbed; on the other was the grass and trees that grew on the hill itself. The patisserie disappeared between them as Cash went, until he turned onto its road.

From this distance, it shone like a beacon, and through the glass, Cash couldn't see anyone. Perhaps they were in the kitchen, or somewhere else in the building. Or maybe the tension of the last few days had made him completely paranoid, and he was being ridiculous thinking this was any kind of breakin plot at all.

Cash parked the SUV next to the road and switched off the lights. It felt a bit silly to be sneaking up on his own business like this, but he had learned to be careful. From here, he still couldn't see anyone. It was making him more hopeful that the lights were an honest mistake rather than something to be alarmed about.

It would be best to enter the building from the kitchen rather than the front. The front doors would make too much noise, and if there was someone there, they'd see him coming from a mile away. From the back, it would be easier to have the element of surprise if he needed it.

Cash thought back to the tension he'd felt when he'd gone to Sigrid's to investigate it on his own. If he hadn't done that, he wouldn't have gotten crucial information that led to the case being solved. And, he had learned a few techniques related to sneaking in the process that were certainly going to help him now.

He slowly made his way toward the back of the building, keeping to the shadows as much as he could. That was difficult, with how clear the night was and how wide the range of the streetlights were. Luckily, there were a few bushes and trees along the way that helped.

After what felt like an eternity, Cash stood outside the back of the patisserie, in the area where the dumpsters were. Ahead, there was the door that led into the kitchen.

He froze for a few moments, straining his ears to listen. He could almost imagine footsteps from inside, but he was fairly sure he wouldn't be able to hear something like that from where he stood.

I just have to get in there and get this over with, he told himself as he gathered all of his courage into a tight bundle in his chest. *Maybe it's nothing and I'm being irrational.*

He wasn't so sure about that, but it was enough to convince himself to take a few steps forward until he stood right outside the door. He shook some of the tension off and reached into his pocket for the key. When he inserted it, he realized that the door had already been unlocked.

"Huh," Cash muttered as he pushed it open and stepped inside. The only people who had keys were the employees; if anyone else had attempted to break in, they would have had to damage the locking mechanisms.

In the kitchen, bent over one of the counters, was Selena. She was hunched down as if she were busy with something important.

"Selena?" Cash asked, surprised that it was her that had made his anxiety run so rampant.

At the sound of his voice, Selena jumped and swung around. For a moment, there was sheer fear in her face, but then she held her hand over her heart, letting go of a few heavy breaths, and laughed.

"Cash!" she said, putting her hands behind her on the counter. "You almost gave me a heart attack!"

"What are you doing here?" Cash was frowning, trying to think of a reason for her to have come to the patisserie after-hours. As far as he knew, Brian and Amelia had everything under control and would have closed up properly.

"Oh, uh..." Selena stood up and crossed her arms. "I was just checking something. I... I thought I left something behind this afternoon, but I guess I didn't, and... Well. I was going to make a quick snack. I'm sorry, I know we're not supposed to do that. I just, I haven't eaten well, and I was so hungry..."

She paused her ramble and looked at Cash sheepishly, as if she were waiting to gauge his reaction.

He was wondering why she hadn't texted him about whatever she'd forgotten, but ascribed it to everything that was going on. As for the snack, that was something that he could easily forgive, especially if she was following the proper safety protocol.

What was odd to him was how flustered and nervous she seemed at getting caught, as if she thought that Cash was going to lose his temper.

Chapter 19

"It's okay, really," Cash reassured Selena, when a movement caught his eye through the small window in the doors that led out to the front of the patisserie. It looked like the headlights of a car, but it had happened fast enough that Cash wasn't sure.

He moved past Selena to open the kitchen doors and spotted the car that was now in the parking lot. It was Susan's. Cash held the doors open, watching her walk up to the front door, and waved before pointing to the left. She got the message and hurried around the building.

Cash turned back to Selena, who was now standing against the counter with crossed arms, looking down at her feet. She looked embarrassed, like a child who had been caught with their hand in the cookie jar. But there was another emotion underneath that, one that Cash couldn't quite put his finger on.

"Just Susan," Cash said, and he noticed Selena lifting her head and tensing her shoulders. They were both very slight movements, and if he hadn't been looking right at her, he wouldn't have seen it.

Cash heard the knock on the kitchen door, and he walked over to open it. Susan stood on the other side, but she hurried past Cash and inside. He closed the door and turned curiously toward her. She seemed not to have even realized that Selena was there, and was somewhat out of breath, as if she had been running.

Susan's eyes carried a look of urgency. She had certainly found something huge and important to the investigation, and Cash felt his heart begin to beat a bit faster.

"I found something," Susan said, confirming what Cash had been thinking. "I was talking to George... And... Orin was allergic to macadamia nuts."

Cash frowned, processing what that could mean. An allergic reaction would explain the lack of blood; it could be quick and almost silent if he went into anaphylactic shock far enough from other people. It would also be difficult to figure out at first glance. But it was something that could be stopped with timely medical intervention; how had it then happened so silently?

"So..." Cash breathed, mulling it over. "He must have been poisoned."

"During the event," Susan added. "That's the only place it could have happened. It would have affected him fast. Probably at the very end."

"He could have been wandering toward the dining room, maybe from the bathroom, struggling to breathe, confused..." Cash muttered, trying to place the puzzle pieces into place in his mind. "It makes sense. But that means that someone involved with the catering had to have done this."

From the corner of his eye, Cash noticed how Selena crossed her arms and how her entire body seemed to tighten. She was glancing past Cash toward the kitchen door, as if she were looking for a way out.

"It could be why Riley arrested Emma," Susan pointed out. "She was directly involved with that, she had access to everything, and she had a motive."

"It wasn't her." Cash turned to face Selena, who was looking more and more like a cornered animal at the other end of the kitchen. She wasn't saying anything, just pushing herself up against the counter as if she could somehow disappear that way.

The realization dawned on Cash in phases as every piece of the evidence came together. The documents with the changed dates and missing names. The fact that Selena had pushed Orin so much all that time ago, and then immediately accused Emma when Orin died. The way she had immediately taken it to the newsletter to convince the rest of the town.

And, the fact that Selena was directly working with the desserts at the brewery event; the last food of the night. Not only that, her section of the recipe was the only one that could have nut extract snuck into it without anyone really noticing. Nobody else would have seen her do it, given how they separated sections of cooking at the patisserie, especially since Cash had been busy elsewhere.

"It was you," Cash breathed, and Selena immediately lifted her hands and shook her head as if she was surprised to be accused of such a thing.

Susan was now staring at Selena openly with a look of shock on her face. "*You* killed him?"

"I don't know what you're talking about," Selena insisted, still shaking her head fervently. "I haven't done anything wrong. He was the closest family I had. Don't you think I want to know who had done this, too? Even the Sheriff knows the truth. You've been blinded by Emma's act."

"No," Cash insisted.

He felt the anger start to bubble up in him, that his own employee would not only betray his friend, but also murder her own family. He was fighting to keep his emotions under control, to keep the situation calm. Somehow, they had to get this information to Riley, without letting Selena get away.

At the same time, there was a cold, numb feeling creeping over him; something that was taking his shock and turning it into focus. It was what he pictured when he'd heard athletes talk about flow state. It was a feeling he was becoming familiar with, and for now, it was a good thing.

It meant that he could focus on getting things done instead of his own emotional reaction to what was going on. For now, Selena couldn't be seen as an employee he was building a connection with. She was a suspect, and he had solid evidence, and that was all that there was. He hoped that Susan could keep her cool as well. This could very easily escalate into something dangerous.

There were a few things they needed to do. First, Selena had to admit what she had done. Secondly, they had to avoid anything becoming violent. And lastly, Cash somehow had to get word to Riley.

"Look," Cash said before Susan could speak, taking one slow step toward Selena with one careful hand up. "This doesn't have to get worse than it is, okay? We already have all of the evidence, Selena. It's only going to end one way."

"It will not," Selena snapped, making Cash back up. This was a kitchen, after all, and there were several things that could become weapons fast. Selena stood close to some of the drawers that held a variety of cutlery; including knives. Cash and Susan wouldn't have much to defend themselves with if it came to that.

"Honestly, a little nut allergy and you think that's what killed him? We barely ever use nuts here anyway." Selena rolled her eyes. "Don't you think there are a million other ways he could've died? How do you even know he was murdered in the first place, huh? Do you have some kind of direct line to the coroner?"

Cash didn't think that Selena would actually attack them; the way that she'd dealt with Orin was planned ahead rather than in the moment. She didn't want to be physically involved. But he needed to be careful. Anything could change within seconds. And it was clear she was becoming erratic; her story kept changing from accusing Emma to questioning whether Orin's death was a murder in the first place.

"We have more than an allergy," Susan said, closing the distance between herself and Selena, too. "There are documents. Right, Cash?"

She looked to him, and he nodded in agreement. "We have the wills that you forged. The fraudulent numbers of the brewery's valuation. The only answer we don't have is *why* you did this now, and not back then."

"I didn't..." Selena muttered, looking away for a moment as if she was thinking about it all. "I didn't do this. I didn't do anything to Arthur's will, and I had nothing to do with property valuations. I'm just a waitress. Why don't you believe me? Why would you believe Emma instead? She has a motive. I don't."

"It all points to you framing her," Cash answered evenly, crossing his arms and holding his ground rather than moving closer and away. From here, it would be difficult for Selena to escape from either of the doors, and all that was behind her was a counter and a jar of cardamom sugar butter. The knives were there, too, but hopefully she wouldn't go that far. This was as safe as the situation could be. "Honestly, why do you think we would underestimate your intelligence like that? *Just a waitress.* You know that's not true."

"Is that why you chose now to do this?" Susan asked, keeping herself slightly behind Cash's left shoulder. "Was this the most convenient time? How long have you been planning this?"

Cash could see that Selena was starting to become nervous. She was fidgeting with her hands and repeatedly switching her weight from one foot to the other. She was getting closer to cracking, he was sure of it.

"It probably was because of convenience," Cash agreed with Susan, building up more pressure. "It was easy to pin this on someone else. You've been waiting to do this for years, haven't you? To murder your own cousin in cold blood, because you didn't get the inheritance you wanted."

"That's not true!" Selena shrieked, balling both hands into fists. "That's not what happened at all!"

"Then what *did* happen?" Cash asked without raising his voice. He realized that she had already made the switch from denial to admitting that she was guilty. "Did you just hate Emma so much that you wanted her to suffer? Is that why you took an innocent life?"

"He wasn't innocent!" Selena insisted. Now, she ran a hand through her hair in frustration. "You have no idea what you're talking about."

"Then tell us," Susan said in return, her answer coming so fast that it almost caught Cash off guard as much as Selena. "Why? Were you caught up in something bigger? What did he do to deserve this?"

"I told you, I didn't..." Selena stopped in the middle of her sentence, staring the two of them down.

Cash and Susan didn't move. It felt as if the room itself was holding its breath. Selena's eyes were burning with fury, but Cash could see something shift in them. He was sure that he was seeing her make a decision; one that could tip everything one way or the other.

"He was going to come clean," Selena breathed, rubbing her face with one hand as if she was exhausted. "He was serious about the transparency thing. He was going to tell everyone *everything.* But he promised. He'd always promised it would go to his grave. That he'd rather die than admit it. He betrayed me."

"What was he going to admit to?" Cash asked, refusing to relent on the pressure. It wasn't a confession yet, but it was almost there. She was already saying more than she should have if she'd wanted to get away with this.

Selena sighed deeply, and Cash noticed a muscle jumping in her jaw. She was looking away from them now, at something or nothing, like she was lost in thought. Cash and Susan both simply waited, even though the tension in the atmosphere was growing with every passing second. There was a tear in Selena's eye, but one that seemed like it could have been conjured up, or simply from frustration.

"We were supposed to be partners in running the brewery," Selena finally said. "We would have inherited it together, sold it, and shared the profits. But Arthur insisted he needed the money, and he knew Emma would take good care of it."

It seemed as if she was talking more to herself than anyone else. Like she was voicing a silent frustration that she'd been carrying all of these years.

"He had it valuated, and..." she started, but trailed off. "It wasn't much higher than what Emma had offered him for it. He wanted to accept it. But that was crazy. It was worth more, and we knew it."

"So, you forged a new number?" Susan asked, one eyebrow raised and a tense chord in her voice.

"A more accurate number," Selena countered snappily, glaring at Susan. "A better number. One that took into consideration all the years that our family put into the place."

Cash didn't mention it, but he found it ironic that Selena would put so much emphasis on her family's contributions when she herself simply wanted to sell the brewery in the first place. It seemed like all she wanted was more money, and not getting it was enough to justify crime. Then, silence was worth murder.

"What happened?" Cash asked.

"We were going to prove that Uncle Arthur was losing his marbles with those documents," Selena answered, chewing at the inside of her cheek like she was fighting to keep her cool. "But Orin backed out at the last minute, when Arthur offered him the shack. It was making good profits, and that was enough for him. I was going to do it by myself, but Orin hid everything from me. He said it was for the best. That we'd make a different plan to get ahead."

"And that ruined your life?" Cash added a dash of compassion into his questioning now, changing the angle to keep her talking. He was releasing the pressure just a little bit, trying to convince her that he had empathy for her situation.

"*Yes,*" Selena almost hissed, though it seemed like she had some sense of relief that Cash was finally listening. Something nobody ever did for her. "I've been stuck in menial jobs ever since, when I was meant to be a millionaire. Everything had been filed. Everything had been in place, and Orin betrayed me."

"He didn't give you anything?" Susan asked, clearly catching on to Cash's strategy. She remained slightly behind him for her own safety, but her voice was filled with confidence.

"Twenty percent of the shack's shares to keep my mouth shut," Selena huffed indignantly, like that was some great disservice. "Barely enough for my house. Can you believe it? Ridiculous. But I agreed to stay silent, and so did he. Neither of us could afford the legal trouble if anyone found out."

"But then he wanted to be mayor," Cash led her further down that hole. They were so close to the confession. She needed to say it.

"And he decided to tell the truth, despite what it would cost?" Susan added.

"He was an idiot. We would have lost everything. He had to go." Selena muttered, turning away from her to splay her hands on the counter.

Cash noticed the cardamom butter there again, and it clicked in his mind. "You poisoned the cardamom butter with macadamia extract, didn't you?"

Selena gave a small nod, enough confirmation that Cash's guess was correct.

"Look, Selena," Cash said, watching her closely for any sudden movements. "It's over now. You should give yourself up."

"Nothing's over."

Chapter 20

As soon as Selena uttered those words, Cash felt a cold sensation travel through his entire body. It slithered through his veins like a snake and made him swallow back the sudden spike in anxiety. It seemed as if Selena's control over her own mind was slipping with every moment that passed.

Selena began to laugh; a dry, bitter sound without any happiness in it. It was like something that she had held within herself for a long time escaping from its cage. It seemed to fill the kitchen with hollow dread, even darkening the lights above.

Cash put his arm in front of Susan, and they took a single step backward, slowly. This was becoming more dangerous, and it was clear that Selena was on the verge of some kind of breakdown. Her entire life was going to crumble down around her far more than it would have if she'd allowed Orin to speak; but somehow, Cash didn't think that she would see it that way.

"You know," Selena said, letting her fingers run over the counter while she still faced away. "I never wanted to have to go this far."

Cash and Susan both stayed silent. Perhaps it was better to let Selena talk. She could incriminate herself even further. Also, at the very least, it would give them a bit of time to come up with a plan if everything went south from here. She seemed to be in her own little world now, like she was talking to a mirror.

"The thing is, everyone knows that I'm not someone who gives up easily," Selena continued in a monotone voice. "I've always given my all when I decide to do something, and this is no different. I tried to talk some sense into Orin, I really did. He wouldn't listen."

She scoffed and shook her head. "He was always so stubborn."

It seemed ironic to call Orin stubborn when Selena was the one who had taken things so incredibly far. She seemed so committed to her own emotions and plans that absolutely nothing could get in her way. Orin was likely trying to change her mind about several things, and she simply refused to listen to him. He had become an inconvenience to her, one that had to be erased entirely.

Cash felt Susan gently squeeze his wrist. They were on the same page. They needed to do something before Selena went over the edge. But what? There was nothing that they could use to trap her or tie her up. There were important documents in the office that Cash didn't want her to get to. Some of the copies of what Lucas had found, and some of Sigrid's original recipes that Cash had been studying. So, locking Selena in there was not an option, either.

"I tried everything. I reminded him that Arthur wouldn't want this," Selena mused, though Cash had the feeling that Arthur was the kind of man who would have preferred the truth over a closet full of family skeletons. Then again, Albert had pointed out that they had many, enough that he no longer wanted to associate with them. Perhaps their family tradition was to keep secrets, and it was something that Orin was going against.

"I told him that he wouldn't get elected, that he'd go to jail. Everything. Not for a second did he even consider what I was saying. One-track minded, just like the rest of them."

Cash started to back away more, separating himself from Susan, who still had an open line to the kitchen door from where she stood. Susan kept her eyes on him while he continued to stare at Selena's back. If she moved, he would be ready. In the meantime, he was thinking of a plan.

"I knew there was no real evidence," Selena went on, throwing her head back for a moment and taking a deep breath. "Well, there *was,* but a little burst pipe eroded it all long ago. Or so I thought. I followed him one day, and I saw where he hid it all."

Cash hadn't even connected those dots. He hadn't thought that something like that could have been done on purpose. But how would Selena even get access to that pipe? It was a question that would likely plague him for a while, but at this point, not one that was important to ask.

While Selena was still looking away from him, he patted his pocket to check that his phone was there. The best thing to do now was to get Riley on the scene as quickly as possible.

Cash didn't know how much time they had to do that, and he could already feel the blood pulsing in his head from the adrenaline. Every movement now had to be calculated and precise.

He had to choose his moment wisely.

"And you know what?" Selena made a fist on the counter. "It's always been like this. I've been giving everything I have every day since I was born, and life constantly throws it back in my face. They always hated me. Every single one of them."

They had to keep her talking, and Cash decided to ask another question. "Really? What's happened to you?"

He laced his voice with a curious compassion that he didn't really mean, but hoped would convince Selena. It seemed like it did when she sighed and turned in his direction slightly, now standing sideways against the counter rather than facing it. She still had her back to Susan, who stole glances at Cash and the back door time and again.

"Too much," Selena finally replied. "I have never gotten what I wanted. No. What I *deserved.* Even when I was a child. My brother got everything handed to him. Same with my cousins. Me? Hand-me-downs, 'that's-nice-dear' comments on my achievements. They got praise, presents, everything."

Cash kept his eyes on her, moving inch by inch to get behind a different counter. If he managed that, half of his body would be hidden, and he'd have his chance to text Riley.

"That doesn't sound fair."

"It wasn't!" Selena snapped again this time, and it was clear that she was falling deeper into some kind of instability. "I was always told about how independent I was, that I didn't need as much encouragement as they did, that excellence was expected from me, not a surprise."

"Did they use those same arguments when it came to your inheritance?" Cash wondered, hoping that this wouldn't push her too far over the edge. He hadn't thought about whether Selena ended up inheriting anything at all, whether from Arthur or anyone else. It wasn't something he particularly had time to look into before, or something that he'd even thought of.

"Ah, yes." Selena laughed that dry laugh again. "The others needed more support. I could make my own way in the world. Not being tied down would set me free to do whatever I wanted in life. Didn't even consider that maybe, just maybe, that little leg-up was something I needed, too."

Cash didn't point out that Orin had, in fact, given her a leg-up with the shares of the fishing shack that he'd given her. There were probably other instances that she overlooked with the tunnel vision that she had. But just pointing this out would probably escalate the situation. They had to keep pretending to be on her side, at least until they could get themselves out—and until they were sure she was in custody.

Finally, Cash made it behind the counter and put his hand in his pocket slowly. He couldn't move too fast.

He noticed Susan glancing at him from the corner of his eye and nodded toward her.

She understood what he was asking instantly and decided to be the one who asked the next question. "Nobody else in the family helped you? Your parents? George?"

"Only if I begged and pleaded, and never like they helped the others," Selena answered, this time turning toward Susan. It was what Cash had been waiting for. He pulled his phone from his pocket, trying not to make any noise. "I confronted them once, but they denied it all. Of course, they did. Narcissists and manipulators, the lot of them. Orin was the only one who ever felt bad for it."

"I didn't know that," Susan said, prompting Selena to sigh and shake her head. It was a melodramatic movement, as if she believed she was the main character in a movie. The overacting would have been humorous if the context wasn't so terrible.

"No one did," she spat. "They're so good at hiding it, just like Emma."

Cash felt a twinge of anger, but he suppressed it quickly. He glanced down at his phone and unlocked it before opening his messages. Then, he had to look back up, to make sure that Selena hadn't noticed.

"She should have been in jail a long time ago," Selena continued furiously, her face starting to turn red. "She stole our family's legacy, no matter what anyone says. I didn't frame her. I just proved her true colors in a way that everyone could understand."

Selena still had her eyes on Susan, burning with a dangerous fire. Cash had the urge to move quicker than he was, but he had to be steady. One mistake could be deadly.

He found Riley's chat—nothing exciting, just a message about meeting sometime for coffee—and looked up just as Selena turned. Now, he was in her sight again. She seemed not to have realized that he'd been looking down, but that wasn't much of a relief. It would be far harder now to send that text. Luckily, he had the messages open. He just had to type and send and hope for the best. But she had to be distracted enough before he could do that.

"Lucas fell for it harder than anyone," Selena went on, a touch of jealousy in her tone that was unexpected. "I warned him, before they even got engaged, but he didn't want to hear me. Why will no one listen to me?"

Her voice was rising, both in volume and tone. She stomped one foot like a toddler about to throw a tantrum. Susan stepped in once again, making Cash incredibly grateful that she'd arrived when she did. He wasn't entirely sure that he would have been able to deal with this on his own.

"We're listening," Susan assured Selena, who now had tears in her eyes. "We're here."

"It's too late now," Selena cried out, fidgeting with the edge of her shirt. "I've gone my whole life in the shadows, and it took going this far for someone to finally *notice?*"

The last word was said in a high pitch, almost like a cymbal crashing at the end of a chaotic symphony.

Cash took that moment to start typing, grateful that he'd shut off button sounds on his phone. He was extra cautious about it, deliberating tapping each letter with slow, hopeful precision. It was difficult without seeing, but he didn't care about spelling or grammar in that moment.

All he needed was for Riley to understand that he was in danger and that he was at the patisserie. Even so, the process was painfully slow. Letter by letter, watching Selena with each press he made on the screen.

"Why did it take so much?" Selena continued, her voice starting to sound strangled. "Why did I have to poison Orin for *someone* to see me? I had to sacrifice the only one who ever tried to help me, because he didn't listen either!"

That was it. A confession, straightforward and with the right wording. It would still only be the word of witnesses, but it was enough for now. She had said it once; if Riley played it right, she would say it again. Even if the physical evidence wasn't damning enough, this would be.

"But it had to be done, you understand?" Selena dropped her voice again this time. The constant movement in her tone and body language showed just how erratic she was becoming. "He betrayed me. He promised he wouldn't say anything. But he was going to, at his next rally. I knew that he would. He told me I'd be alright, but I knew I wouldn't."

Premeditated then, Cash thought as he finally typed the last word and sent the message with a quick glance down to make sure he found the right button.

"Selena," Cash said, hoping that her name would pull her back in the direction of calm. "We can help you. We want to. You just need to—"

"No!" she snapped, then drifted into a tense, unsettling silence. Her eyes were growing wild, and it was intense enough for Cash to take a step backward from where he stood. Susan, too, was now backing away, toward the kitchen door.

Selena's breath grew heavier, her shoulders pulled up as she stared them down. "You know, I am sorry that it has come to this."

Neither Cash nor Susan said anything, waiting for the penny to drop.

"But you two have heard too much."

Chapter 21

"Wait," Cash said, taking another step back, in Susan's direction. He shielded her with one hand, while the other was held out in front of him. "You don't want to do this."

"I never got anywhere doing the right thing," Selena replied calmly, squaring her shoulders and crossing her arms. "I have no choice anymore. I want a life outside of being a damn baker."

"I thought you'd need time to grieve," Cash answered, filling his words with sympathy rather than the anxiety that was starting to build. "It was never going to be permanent."

"You didn't trust me to handle it myself!" Selena hissed at him. "You thought I was too weak, didn't you? Admit it!"

It seemed as if she still thought herself on the right side of morality, despite everything that she had done. Her mind had clearly become twisted from years of resentment slowly building into a horrifying crescendo. Cash couldn't imagine ever thinking that murder was justified, but in Selena's mind, it was a necessary evil.

"I understood what it was like to lose someone," Cash retorted. "I knew how difficult it was to go through something like that."

He didn't add that he hadn't been the one to commit the murder in the first place. It made him wonder whether any of the emotions he had seen in Selena until that evening had been real, or simply a performance. How deep had her manipulation and delusions truly gone?

"You understand nothing." Selena started pulling at the drawer closest to her, probably looking for a weapon.

Susan grasped at Cash's arm. He knew that it was probably time to get out of there, but that would give Selena a chance to escape. And who knew what she could do to people in the town if she did? What if she chased them? Here, at least, there were lights, and they would be able to react.

Plus, Cash hoped that Riley was on his way. That he would be there in time. Lucas and Kieran were coming, too. Between all of them, they would be able to subdue her.

He needed to win just a little bit more time, no matter what he had to do to get it. But he didn't want Susan to get hurt because of that. He glanced at her and nodded toward the door, but she shook her head. Clearly, if he was going to stay, then she would, too. It was admirable, but not the smartest choice. Even so, Cash wouldn't push her. He had to keep Selena from attacking.

"We can talk about this," Cash said to Selena, who was still rifling through the drawer. "I'll make us a coffee, and we can sit in the front. We can figure it out, together. It doesn't have to be this way, Selena."

Before Selena could answer, they all heard the screech of two sets of tires outside. Two vehicles had arrived.

The moment paused the chaos in the kitchen, with Selena, Cash, and Susan all turning their heads toward the source of the sound. There was a rush, and another crash; the front glass doors being broken in with impressive force.

"I told you!" Lucas's voice rang out through the air that now flowed through the patisserie. "I told you that Emma was innocent, and you didn't want to hear it! *Apologize!*"

"Lucas, we really don't have time for this," Riley's answer came tersely, amid the crunching of broken glass under boots and shoes. "We don't know what's going on in there, either. You should stay back."

"I will not!" Lucas yelled furiously. "Cash is my friend, too! Who knows what you'll do to him. Are you taking him down for nothing, too?"

While they argued, it seemed like Selena had found what she had been looking for. She pulled a knife from the drawer and placed the tip against one finger. She stared down at it as she played with it, a new expression growing on her face. It had a serrated blade; more useful for slicing bread than anything else, but it could certainly do catastrophic damage in the hands of a maniac.

"I'll tell them it was self-defense," she muttered in between the yells from the front of the patisserie. "You two accused me of murder, you attacked me, and I had to save myself."

"Put it down," Susan said, though the usual confident authority in her voice had disappeared. "Selena, you're making a mistake, and you know it."

"I don't think so."

Then Selena lunged forward, the knife gripped tightly in her hand.

For Cash, the world seemed to slow down to a crawl in that moment. He opened his mouth and shouted. His voice came out raw and primal, with a powerful tone that surprised him.

"Riley! She has a knife!"

Immediately, he pulled Susan toward the kitchen door. The argument at the front of the patisserie stopped, and he heard footsteps running. He wondered for a moment who would have joined, but realized that it must have been Kieran, given that he'd been with Lucas at the library.

Selena swung the knife, but missed by inches. She raised her arm again while Cash grabbed the handle of the back door. He saw Riley, Lucas, and Kieran burst through the other door behind Selena. Lucas and Kieran stayed back when Riley lunged forward.

"Sheriff! Drop your weapon!" Riley yelled, but Selena didn't even seem to hear him. She still moved forward, toward Cash and Susan.

Cash managed to throw the kitchen door open, and he and Susan tumbled outside. He heard a click and the sound of electricity. Selena, still clutching the knife, went down, shaking as the taser's current went through her.

"Let go of it," Riley said, stepping forward and kicking at the knife. Selena, however, did not seem to want to give up, even now.

She rolled over and pushed herself up on her hands and knees. "Why? Why are all of you doing this to me? What is your problem?"

"Drop your weapon," Riley ordered again, standing between her and Lucas and Kieran.

Cash held his ground with Susan behind him, ready to move if he needed to. Selena was breathing heavily, her hair obscuring the view of her face. It was almost impossible to tell what she was thinking.

In a flash, she was somehow on her feet again, screaming something incoherent. It was like watching her turn into a wild animal, a far cry from the slightly temperamental but controlled woman Cash thought she was. She had lost so much of her humanity to pure emotion that it was frightening. Cash and Riley moved forward at the same time.

Cash smacked at her hand, loosening her grip on the knife. It clattered to the ground loudly. Riley grabbed her by the arms and swung her around, keeping her wrists together at her back. Susan stepped forward to kick the knife well out of reach, but stayed out of the way of the main struggle. Riley used one elbow to push Selena downward so that she was bent over the counter in front of her.

"Stop!" Selena screamed. "You're ruining everything! You should be arresting *them*!"

"You're under arrest for assault with a deadly weapon," Riley said, loudly, but calmly. "If you resist, you'll have another charge added to that. Think about what you're doing, Selena."

Riley kept holding her with one hand, while the other reached for the handcuffs on his belt. In that moment, Selena ripped herself out of his grip and pushed herself away from the counter. She ran for the front of the store, but Lucas and Kieran immediately stopped her. Each grabbed an arm and held on for dear life.

"Get down!" Riley commanded as Selena continued to try and wrestle herself free. Between Kieran and Lucas, they managed to get her to the ground, and Riley perched on top of her as they forced her arms back. "Stop resisting!"

Selena shrieked and wiggled, but between the three of them, they managed to keep her down for Riley to get the handcuffs on her wrists. He sat back, still covering her legs, while she continued to fight. It looked like he was waiting for her to run out of steam before he tried to get her to her feet again.

Cash watched. But he did feel relieved that he and Susan were safe now, that nobody else would get hurt in the middle of this chaos.

Selena finally stopped, out of breath and looking disheveled. Cash heard her begin to sob as Riley got up and forced her to her feet. She looked at the floor, her shoulders shaking.

He did hope that she had given up at this point, so that this whole night could be over with.

"Why won't you listen to me?" Selena cried as Riley began leading her past Lucas and Kieran and toward the front of the patisserie.

Everyone else followed, not out of curiosity but because no one seemed to know what else to do.

"They're all lying," Selena continued, with Riley simply moving ahead in complete silence. "All of you have been against me from the start! You're all on *her* side! Throwing me under the bus for a monster!"

Nobody replied to her. Her voice was the only thing ringing out through the night. Cash noticed Susan shaking beside him, the effects of adrenaline likely starting to wear off at this point. Cash's own hands felt somewhat clammy, and he noticed how hard his heart had been beating. His mind wasn't processing what had happened yet, still protecting him from panic.

Lucas moved a few feet closer to Riley's truck, though still keeping a bit of space from it. His body was tense, as if he was ready to jump into action if Selena tried anything again. At this point, however, it looked as if her body had used every ounce of adrenaline-fueled energy that she had. Her shrieks were still ringing out over the world, but she looked exhausted. There wasn't much she would be able to do at this point, even if she did manage to get loose from her handcuffs.

Riley opened the truck door while Selena continued to scream about how no one was listening to her and everyone was against her. She continued blaming Cash and Susan for what was happening, continued to insist that Emma was the truly guilty party, and continued to complain about her own issues. Cash started letting most of it fade away, having heard enough from her in the kitchen already.

"Get in," Riley said firmly, but Selena was still struggling against him. "You're only going to get more charges. Why are you trying to make this so much worse than it needs to be?"

He started bundling her into the backseat, but she still continued to yell over his shoulder. "You think what I did to Orin was the last of it? You'll see, you'll get your consequences! I'll get you back for this—all of you!"

Riley paused there for a moment, noting her confession, but then continued to get her into the car. He folded her in from her middle, expert movements that showed the intensity of his training. Finally, her head disappeared, and Riley slammed the door, muffling her screams.

Chapter 22

From where Cash stood, he could still see Selena thrashing inside of the patrol truck, but he could no longer hear her. He felt his shoulders drop and let out a breath he hadn't realized he had been holding.

"Are you okay?" Cash asked Susan, who was still tightly gripping his arm. Her face was pale and her eyes wide and she was breathing shallow and fast. She seemed to realize how tightly she was holding on to him, and released him before putting her hands together in front of her.

"I... I think so," she said with a meek nod. "You?"

"I'm fine," Cash answered, trying to smile, though it faltered somewhat. "Lucas? Kieran? No injuries?"

Kieran only shook his head. Lucas was still staring at Riley, who was approaching the group. Cash knew that Lucas's anger might still be growing now that the real suspect was in custody. However, he also hoped that

Lucas would be able to keep it under control while Riley was trying to sort all of this out.

"I've got this under control now," Riley said when he reached them. "I'll talk to you all at the station in the morning. I think it would be better if you all went home."

Cash noticed Riley looking at him in particular, with a mix of slight disappointment and concern. Riley studied him subtly, but closely, likely looking for any injuries.

Lucas stepped forward to speak, but Riley held up a hand. "You are welcome to pick up Emma from the station. She will be free to go, no charges."

"There never should have been an arrest in the first place," Lucas growled in return.

Luckily, he did not continue with their previous argument. Having another disagreement after all of that chaos would have been too much. They were all completely exhausted, barely even able to keep themselves standing.

The air was still electrified, but it was slowly cooling down. Cash could feel the aftershock settling in as the adrenaline faded away, and he was certain he'd have a headache soon. He definitely needed something with sugar in it and a strong mug of coffee.

"We found evidence in the archives," Kieran pointed out. "We'll gather it together and drop it off in the morning. You know, if that'll help."

He added a bit of a nonchalant shrug to his last words. Riley chuckled dryly and shook his head before he looked over at Cash.

"What about the tie?" Cash asked, remembering that it had been missing. "Orin's? It was gone."

"It had been thrown under a chair. He probably took it off while he was struggling to breathe." Riley reached out with one hand and let his fingers lightly touch Cash's arm and winked at him. "If I didn't know any better, I'd have sworn that you were trying to steal my job."

Cash had to look away as he felt his cheeks heating up and turning red. "I just wanted to help."

"Uh-huh," Riley said, though he didn't sound as angry as Cash would have expected him to be. "Well, I have to get Selena down to the station and into a holding cell. She'll have a chance to calm down in there. Don't worry, you're all safe. There's enough from the investigation and the scene to prove homicide by anaphylactic shock. We found Orin's EpiPen in the dumpster behind the brewery, too. I've sent it for fingerprint testing, and I have a feeling it will come back a match for Selena."

"Thank you," Cash said, turning back to offer Riley a sincere smile. "I don't know what we would have done if you weren't here."

"Don't mention it," Riley answered, before he glanced at everyone else and cleared his throat. "Uhm... Please report to the station in the morning. I'm going to need statements from all of you. And, well, that evidence you mentioned, Kieran. I'm sure it will be helpful. Lucas, we'll be waiting for you."

Everyone nodded, shock setting in properly now. Riley turned back to his old truck and began to walk toward it. Cash couldn't help but watch him go; the way he held his shoulders, his powerful stride. He had a quiet strength in everything that he did, something that was comforting in a situation like this.

Lucas followed, too, moving to his van in a purposeful hurry. He was clearly only thinking about one thing: getting Emma out of that jail cell and back home.

The rest of them stood frozen while Riley and Lucas reached their vehicles, got in, and drove away. It was like nobody really knew what to do now that the craziness was over with.

Cash decided that maybe it was best if he took the lead from here. "Do you want something to drink? Tea, coffee?"

Kieran and Susan looked at one another, then both muttered a "yes." Cash assumed that they'd prefer something with a bit of a kick, and made the decision that he'd make the patisserie's strongest coffee for all of them.

"Right, please, come in," Cash said, before making a small joke to try and lighten the mood. "Please excuse all of the broken glass. We've had a minor incident."

Kieran scoffed a laugh at that, more surprised than genuine amusement, but Susan only smiled slightly. Kieran led her to a corner table while Cash headed for the kitchen, his eyes trailing the shards of glass that were now on the floor. He tried to avoid them, but heard a few crunches from his shoes as he walked.

Cash caught a glimpse of his own face in one of the broken windows and noticed that he seemed somewhat pale. It wasn't surprising; even if this was his second time dealing with a murderer, it seemed, somehow, to have been far more dangerous than before.

Selena had been working right alongside him, Brian, and Amelia for over a month. Years before that she'd spent working under Sigrid. She had a bright future in the industry, and Cash had even considered letting her take a majority of the managerial duties. He'd had no idea what she was truly capable of, and hadn't had any idea she'd been planning something like this.

Don't think about it right now, he reminded himself, knowing full well that he could easily let his thoughts spiral. He was still dealing with Sigrid's death and everything that had happened then; letting it all compound right now could break him.

He was shaking as he switched on the coffee machine and gathered three mugs. It felt strange to be making coffee under the circumstances, but at the same time, it was something normal, something that he could focus on without giving in to the panic that still hovered over him.

Cash listened to the noises of the machine, focusing on every crackle and droplet. It was a technique he'd heard of somewhere and had been using whenever he thought too deeply of Sigrid. For now, it was good enough, and it helped his nerves somewhat. He had to be strong for the others, make sure that they were alright. Once the dust had settled and he was back home, that was when he could let himself decompress.

Once the coffee was ready, Cash put them all on a tray and carried them out to the front. Kieran and Susan were seated against the opposite wall, as far from the broken doors as they could get.

To Cash, the sight was fairly bizarre. Seeing the patisserie with broken windows was strange. He trembled as he walked past, trying his best to keep his eyes on the booth where Susan and Kieran were seated. Susan was staring at the table, while Kieran had his hand on her shoulder.

Cash placed a coffee in front of each of them before he sat down across from Susan. He stirred his own coffee as the silence between them grew.

"Susan, are you alright?" Cash eventually asked, and she lifted her head tiredly.

"I think so," she said, though her voice was shaky. "I'm just... I can't believe that just happened. I've known Selena since she was a little girl. I never thought she'd be capable of something so terrible, you know?"

"Yeah," Cash agreed with a deep sigh. "I didn't notice a single sign. They must have been there, right?"

"Hindsight is twenty-twenty," Kieran pointed out, starting to stir his own coffee with the spoon that Cash had placed in it. It wasn't doing much, but it was something to fidget with. "It's not either of your faults. You couldn't have seen this coming."

Cash knew that was true, but somehow he still blamed himself. He'd always thought of himself as observant, and through his investigations, there was definitely evidence of that. But he hadn't seen Selena's dark side, even for a second. He hadn't even considered her a suspect, even when he was looking at Orin's family.

"At least it's all over now," Susan breathed, sitting back against the booth. "I'm just glad you all arrived when you did. I was... so terrified."

"Me, too," Cash admitted, putting his hand on hers. "But we're safe. Nothing else is going to happen. Emma will go home, and Selena will face justice. You'll see. Everything will be alright."

Cash said it with conviction, but it was as much to convince himself as it was to convince Susan. He wasn't sure how he'd feel when he was home alone again. Physically, he was safe. That much was true. But mentally and emotionally, he wasn't sure how long it would take to recover this time.

"We found her," Kieran said with a dry laugh. "It was because of us that she got caught in the first place. I know it's hard to do right now, but that's something to celebrate."

"You're right," Susan replied, straightening herself up in her chair and fixing her hair. She grasped the handle of her mug and lifted it. "To catching our man. Woman. You know what I mean."

Cash chuckled and lifted his mug, as did Kieran. The three of them clinked all their mugs together in a strange toast, and each took a sip of the warm coffee inside. It was sweet, filled with sugar; Cash remembered Sigrid saying that it would help with shock when he was younger. He wasn't sure if there was a scientific basis for that in the slightest, but that didn't matter.

"Thank you both for helping me," Cash said, staring at his own mug. "Honestly, for believing in me. I could never have done any of this without you. We're a great team."

"I knew your gut would be right." Kieran shrugged as he sipped. Cash smiled. Kieran had truly been a friend from the start. He had already known that he could trust the librarian, but their second case had completely solidified it. Even if the entire town doubted the truth, Kieran would not.

"I had a feeling that there had been something deeper," Susan added. There was a distant look in her eye. "I had racked my brain for days, trying to remember everything about the family. Then, it came to me. An incident at a birthday party I attended many years ago. Orin had a muffin with macadamia nuts in it and had a reaction. It was a whole mess."

"That was literally what we needed to crack the case," Cash murmured.

"I wonder if she'd stolen his EpiPen, too," Kieran mused. "I don't think he was the kind of man who would have gone anywhere without it."

"Riley will probably get that information out of her." Cash took his spoon out of his coffee and stared at his reflection in it for a moment. He found himself wondering, again, why Riley had arrested Emma. Was it only on circumstantial evidence? Was it because it happened in her brewery, and she had a passing connection?

And why had Riley touched his arm like that earlier? It was definitely more than simply a friendly gesture, especially with the wink added.

"I heard there was a commotion here. Police scanners are pretty useful." The new voice made all three of them jump. Pete was peering in through the broken front door, notebook in hand. "Thought it might be worth a front page."

Cash sighed and waved Pete over. "I'll tell you what I can, and nothing else. Are you happy with that?"

"Ah, if it means I can spend a bit of time with you, I'll take it," Pete answered, approaching their table. "I'll keep it simple, if you'd like. Just the where and the who. You don't need to give me any details."

Those statements only served to confuse Cash even further. Riley wasn't the only one tugging at his heart; Pete was, too. Cash didn't really want his love life to be pulling him away from the situation at hand, but maybe a little bit of light-heartedness could be healthy. Then again, was this tug and pull between Pete and Riley really that light-hearted? Frankly, Cash wasn't sure.

But it was better than dealing with another murder. He'd had enough of those for an entire lifetime.

Epilogue

Pete kept his word, only asking a few basic questions before pivoting to asking if they were all alright. He put his notebook away and listened intently with a clear sincerity in his eyes. Eventually, everyone had finished their coffee, and they sat for a while longer before Cash checked his watch.

"Wow, I didn't realize it was that late," he said, running a hand through his hair. "We should all probably get some rest, shouldn't we?"

Kieran, Susan, and Pete all shared a look. Pete spoke first. "Well, I'm pretty sure things are going to be crazy tomorrow. So, that sounds like a good idea to me. I'll reach out to Lucas and Emma for my retraction article. Pretty sure I owe them an enormous apology."

"Mm," Kieran and Susan agreed, though they didn't get up first. Pete stretched himself out and got to his feet, offering a hand to Cash to help him get out of the booth.

Without really thinking about it, Cash accepted the offer. It was only when he was standing beside the booth that he realized what had just happened.

He tried not to think about it too much as Kieran and Susan both got up, too. The four of them walked to the door to get outside, trying to avoid most of the broken glass.

In the parking area, the world was quiet aside from the breeze running through the trees and the sound of the island's insects. Above them, the moon hung high and bright along with the stars. It was a night like any other on Salt Cliff, and if it weren't for the broken doors,

Cash could have easily forgotten everything that had just happened.

"Kieran, do you need a ride?" Susan asked, almost as if she wanted him to agree. Cash could understand that she didn't want to be alone.

He himself needed a bit of space, and couldn't wait to get home, but he still had that distant feeling of imminent danger he hadn't quite let go of yet.

Kieran nodded at Susan, following her to her car and leaving Cash with Pete.

"I'll see you tomorrow, then?" Pete asked, his voice filled with concern. "Will you be fine?"

Cash couldn't help but smile. This was the first time that he'd seen Pete so serious about something. "I'll be okay, don't worry."

He walked away, heading to the SUV. It felt as if the weight of the world was on his shoulders, but he also had a deep sense of relief in his soul. The investigation was finally over, and he'd found the truth. Emma was going to be set free, and they knew who had been behind everything. For now, he could breathe.

Cash took a shower when he got home, and almost immediately crashed into bed and fell asleep. He hadn't expected that sleep would come so easily, but he had been so exhausted from the last few days that his body was grateful for the rest.

He woke to his alarm in the morning, rather than getting up naturally; a rare occurrence even before he had needed to wake up early to bake and open the patisserie.

Wow, I really have been tired, Cash found himself thinking as he stood in front of the mirror to brush his teeth and hair. He didn't really want to have breakfast, but made himself a bowl of cereal anyway. He'd need the energy.

Despite the fact that the arrest had happened and his own investigation was over, there would be a lot of hard work still to do. He needed to make sure people knew Fjord & Fika would be closed again for a few days, get someone to fix the doors, talk to Riley, and check in with Emma, Lucas, Kieran, Susan, Brian, and Amelia. At the moment, it all seemed a bit overwhelming.

One step at a time, Cash reminded himself as he placed his finished bowl in the dishwasher and went to get dressed.

It took about an hour from when he had woken up, but he was finally ready to go. The first stop would be Emma and Lucas's place. He knew it was possible that they'd prefer to be alone for now, but he also had to make sure they were alright, given the circumstances.

He reached their home and stepped out of his SUV, walking up to the front door. A few knocks later, Lucas opened the door and called out for Emma.

She was disheveled when she appeared in the hallway, but as soon as she saw Cash, her face lit up and she rushed at him. She wrapped him up in a tight hug and he could feel her start to sob.

"Thank you," she muttered into his shoulder. "Thank you..."

She repeated the phrase a few more times before pulling away and wiping the tears from her eyes. "I don't know what we would have done without you, Cash, honestly. Thank you."

"Don't mention it," Cash answered almost bashfully, not sure what to do with all of this gratitude. "I'm just glad you got out."

"Riley treated me well enough," Emma said, though a dark cloud moved over Lucas's face at the mention of his name. "I knew I just had to wait. That you would all come through for me. I just... I can't believe Selena was the one who did it in the end."

"Me neither," Cash answered as Emma and Lucas stood to one side to let him in.

"The others are here, too," Emma said with a smile. "I can't believe there were so many people looking out for me."

Cash followed them to the living room, which wasn't a small room, but seemed filled to the brim with everyone inside. Jamie, Kieran, Susan, Pete, Brian, and Amelia were all seated on the various couches and chairs. Kieran made space for Cash and patted the couch next to him.

As Cash took his seat, Lucas walked out of the room, and Emma sat down on the only open chair.

"Cash, you really hit this one out of the park," Kieran chuckled, smacking Cash on the knee. "You should consider a career as a private investigator."

"I had a lot of help," Cash pointed out, looking at each of them in turn. "Without you, I never would have gotten to the bottom of this whole thing. But I'll be honest, it's pretty tiring. I'd prefer it if I didn't have to go around figuring out murders."

"Ah, that's a fair thing to want," Pete said in agreement. "I mean, it's good for reader numbers, but really not particularly pleasant."

"I'm sure things will be back to normal soon," Emma added, putting her hands together in her lap.

Cash wasn't sure that things would ever really be normal on Salt Cliff. In his short time on the island, the drama was second only to the amount of recent murders. He hoped that nothing else of note would happen, at least not soon. All he wanted was to get back to running the patisserie and spending time with his friends, without having to question them about deaths.

Lucas appeared in the doorway with a tray of cups of tea, handing one to each of the people present. Then, he went to stand next to Emma with his hand on her shoulder. He still seemed tense, which made sense to Cash. He probably wasn't very happy with Riley, and clearly worried about his wife.

"What did Riley say about being wrong?" Susan asked Emma, both curious and concerned. "Did he at least admit it?"

"He apologized profusely," Emma answered, playing with the tag on her teabag. "Insisted he didn't know how to make it up to me, and hoped that I would forgive him."

"He shouldn't have done it in the first place," Lucas grumbled. "You didn't deserve to go through that."

Emma looked up at him, her face soft. "He was just doing what he thought was right. I can't really blame him for that. I know it's tough, but that's how things are."

Lucas didn't answer, but Cash noticed a muscle jump in his jaw. It would be a while before he even considered talking to Riley again. That made Cash feel a bit sad. Riley could be somewhat pushed away from his friendships because of Emma's arrest. Cash himself wasn't entirely sure what to feel, either. He knew that he wanted to talk to Riley about it all first; maybe then, he'd have more certainty.

But he'd worry about that when he went down to the station. For now, he was spending time with his friends, and he needed to focus on them. He wanted to make sure that they'll all be alright.

"We'll probably be closed again," Brian said, glancing in Cash's direction. "Can't exactly have customers over with all the broken glass, right?"

Cash assumed that Susan, Lucas, and Kieran had filled the others in on what had happened the previous night. He was somewhat relieved, since he didn't want to rehash it too many times himself. Riley was probably also going to have a slew of questions for him about everything that Selena had said and done.

"At least a week or two," Cash replied. "Probably two. I need a break, and I think you do as well."

"Definitely," Amelia breathed. "Honestly, I don't think there's been this much chaos since my family moved to the island. It's like everything has been happening all at once. I might head to the mainland just to take some time away."

"Good idea," Pete agreed with a laugh. "Maybe we should all take a vacation."

"I'll absolutely be thinking about it," Susan said, though her tone told Cash that she'd likely not leave her post anytime soon. There would probably be another election announced, with the current race being postponed to see if any other candidates would come forward. "Though I do believe that the island might need me now more than ever."

"Yeah," Emma answered, sipping slowly at her own cup of tea before continuing. "I think we'll keep the brewery shut down for at least a month. Maybe take a trip, just the two of us."

"Irene is going to be busy," Kieran added, mentioning the island's therapist, who Cash had been seeing since

Sigrid's passing. "I know I'll be increasing my own appointments for a while."

"So, uh..." Brian shifted in his seat somewhat awkwardly. It looked like he had a burning question on his mind, and when he spoke again, it came right out. "Are you going to get a replacement for Selena soon?"

Cash almost laughed. He hadn't thought about that at length, but it was an obvious step that had to be made. It was strange to think that there was such a sudden void in Sigrid's legacy; one that Cash had not expected. Selena had been one of Sigrid's first apprentices and knew the ins and outs of the patisserie better than almost anyone else. Replacing her was going to be tough, but it was necessary.

"Probably," Cash finally answered. "I just hope whoever I pick is a little less... interesting."

His reply received a round of awkward laughs, but it did manage to break the tension in the room. Cash continued drinking his tea with his friends, the conversation drifting more toward small talk and away from the aftermath of Orin's murder. Eventually, people began to leave one by one, and Cash was one of the last to leave.

He stood outside of Lucas and Emma's home for a minute, calming his mind and wondering whether he'd finally get that relaxed island life he'd hoped for.

Cash thought of Riley and Pete, and everything that had been happening. Relaxed definitely wasn't how he would have described his life on the island so far; but he couldn't deny that it was sure to be interesting.

Lefse With Cardamom Sugar Butter Recipe

Lefse Potatoes Recipe

In my family we love our lefse fresh or from frozen! While different family members have their own special tweaks to the recipe—this is our go to for a delicious treat.

Equipment Needed:

- Large pot—for boiling potatoes
- Potato ricer—essential for smooth, fluffy potatoes
- Mixing bowls—for dough preparation
- Wooden spoon or spatula—for mixing
- Measuring cups & spoons—for accuracy
- Lefse rolling pin (grooved or textured preferred) with a rolling pin cover—this prevents sticking and helps roll thin
- Pastry board or cloth-covered board—floured, for rolling out thin rounds
- Lefse stick (turning stick)—for lifting and flipping without tearing
- Griddle or flat skillet—large, flat, evenly heated surface (traditional lefse griddles are 16–17" round)
- Cooling racks or clean towels—to cool lefse while keeping them soft
- Plastic wrap or zip bags—for storing finished

lefse

Ingredients for Lefse Dough:

- 20 cups riced potatoes (20 cups = 10 lbs)
- 2 eggs
- 2 tsp baking powder
- 1 1/2 tsp salt
- 4 cups flour
- 2 cups melted Crisco

Instructions

Potatoes:

1. Use netted gems or baking type potatoes.
2. Peel and cook potatoes until well done. Do not undercook or add salt to the water.
3. Drain.
4. Rice potatoes.
5. Stir in 2 cups melted Crisco immediately after ricing.
6. Rice again to improve quality.
7. Place riced potatoes in cool place overnight

(e.g., basement floor).

8. Do not refrigerate because texture becomes too hard & wet. Don't pack. Leave fluffy.
9. Cover container with towel.

Lefse:

1. Beat eggs; add baking powder & salt, mix.
2. Mix 2 cups flour with potatoes, then add egg mixture.
3. Use approx. 2 more cups flour while kneading into loaves.
4. Place loaves on cookie sheet.
5. Keep cool in fridge until needed.
6. Preheat lefse griddle to 450°F.
7. Cut off a portion of dough and roll into a slightly larger than a baseball-sized piece. Roll out on a floured pastry board with a lefse rolling pin until very thin (about 1/8 inch).
8. Use a lefse stick to carefully lift the rolled dough and place it onto the hot griddle.
9. Cook until bubbles form and brown spots appear (about 1 minute), then flip with lefse

stick and cook the other side.

10. Transfer cooked lefse to a clean towel, stacking them between layers of towels to cool and keep soft.
11. Once cooled, store lefse in plastic wrap or zip bags to maintain freshness.

Cardamom Sugar Butter (Large Batch)

(enough for "quality control tasting")

Ingredients:

- 1 cup (2 sticks) salted butter, room temperature
- ½ cup granulated sugar
- 2 tablespoons brown sugar
- 2 to 3 teaspoons ground cardamom, to taste
- **Vanilla option:** 1 teaspoon vanilla bean paste *(or ½ teaspoon vanilla extract if needed, but*

Cash insists the paste is better)

Instructions:

1. Beat the softened butter until light and creamy.
2. Add both sugars and the cardamom; mix until fully blended and fluffy.
3. Stir in vanilla bean paste until speckles are evenly distributed.
4. Taste and adjust—if the cardamom doesn't sing when tasting, add another pinch.
5. Keep covered at room temperature during serving so it spreads smoothly.

To Serve:

- Spread generously over warm lefse, reaching all the way to the edges.
- Roll tightly from one side, press gently to seal, and serve immediately.
- (My family says the end piece is the baker's

tax.)

Storage

- Keeps 1 week in the refrigerator
- Freeze up to 2 months—thaw at room temperature before using

www.ingramcontent.com/pod-product-compliance
Lightning Source LLC
LaVergne TN
LVHW091111080826
845145LV00008B/1871

* 9 7 8 1 0 6 9 1 4 3 4 3 3 *